A CRY
FROM THE GRAVE

"She was killed around 10:30 this morning," said Detective Cunningham. "This is the murder weapon. We found it beside the body."

He lifted a plastic bag with a small tag on it. I saw the quartz-bladed knife and couldn't take my eyes off it. There was a disturbing aura coming from the weapon that drew me perversely, even as I tried to keep myself aloof.

I held out my hands and Cunningham dropped the blade flat across my palms.

The knife screamed and screamed and screamed ... the sound of agonizing death.

Other Avon Books by
Robert E. Vardeman

ANCIENT HEAVENS

THE SCREAMING KNIFE

ROBERT E. VARDEMAN

AVON BOOKS ◆ NEW YORK

AVON BOOKS
A division of
The Hearst Corporation
105 Madison Avenue
New York, New York 10016

Copyright © 1990 by Robert E. Vardeman
Front cover photograph by Walter Wick
Published by arrangement with the author
Library of Congress Catalog Card Number: 89-92499
ISBN: 0-380-75856-3

First Avon Books Printing: August 1990

AVON TRADEMARK REG. U.S. PAT. OFF. AND IN OTHER COUNTRIES, MARCA REGISTRADA, HECHO EN U.S.A.

Printed in the U.S.A.

RA 10 9 8 7 6 5 4 3 2 1

For those who shine the light along
the dark, mysterious paths:

Tony Hillerman
Lois Duncan
and
R. D. Brown

CHAPTER ONE

"I'm sorry we have to use this room," the woman said. "The others were in use." She cinched the straps around my bare chest until I gasped. "Too tight? Sorry," she said, not meaning it. She made no move to loosen the heavy metal-studded leather bands.

I tried to turn and see what she did at the table behind me. The clamps on my head kept me from turning. I had to stare straight ahead at the pale green wall. I swallowed hard. Tiny spots of blood still dotted an area about three feet off the floor.

"I don't want him moving when we turn on the juice to the head electrodes," came a heavier, huskier voice. I caught movement out of the corner of my left eye.

"Who are you?" I asked. I knew the woman slightly—Barbara Chan. But the man was an unknown. Pain shot through my upper arms as the woman, now dressed in a white lab coat, applied the electrodes to my biceps. She continued to work as the man came to stand in front of me.

He glowered, his dewlaps quivering. "David Michaelson. And we're supposed to ask the questions."

"You're personally doing this?" I asked. My mouth was turning dry. From the corner of my right eye I saw a gurney being pushed into another room. The body on it was draped with a soiled white sheet. The doors slammed loudly behind the vanishing cadaver.

"Let's get this over. I think it's a waste of time," Michaelson said to Barbara Chan.

The woman looked up into my eyes. A smile danced on her lips. "This is sort of . . . sexy," she said too softly for Michaelson to hear. I didn't answer, even when her hand lightly brushed over my lap. I was just glad she didn't fasten an electrode there.

"Focus on the spot on the wall," she said. A tight, eye-searing dot of white tried to peel off the pastel paint. I couldn't look at it; my eyes kept drifting to the blood stains.

"Equipment is up to power," came Michaelson's cold voice. I jerked when electric surges danced into my body.

"Sorry," he said. He lied and we both knew it. The man worked a few more seconds at the bank of equipment I knew had to line the wall behind me.

"This won't take long," Barbara Chan said. I couldn't tell if she was speaking to me or Michaelson. And it didn't matter. I wanted it to be over. The straps cut off my circulation, the tiny pulses of energy gamboling along my flesh distracted me—and promised real pain—and the spot of light was giving me a headache.

"Concentrate," the woman told me. "Concentrate and let's begin."

I began breathing slowly, deeply, letting the oxygen flow through my body. The tight straps receded in importance. I forgot about the electrodes. Even the hot white spot faded from my vision.

Barbara Chan walked around in front of me. She carried a long-handled shovel. She bounced it in her hands, as if it were a baseball bat and she was measuring its weight before the home run swing. She thrust it toward me. Although the leather straps around my upper arms restrained movement, I was able to take the shovel, both hands on the handle.

I screamed as electricity volted through me. My back tried to arch, then break. Blackness sucked at my soul and drew me down into it. And there was more, too much more.

Itching. Terrible prickling. The itching on my forehead and arms intensified until I wanted to cry out. Flesh began peeling off my face in huge chunks. Blood ran into my eyes and blinded me. And agony! The awful pain!

Worse than this soul-searing pain was the blackness drifting inexorably toward me. It billowed around me, an inky fog worse than any slipping silently through the Golden Gate and covering San Francisco Bay like a shroud. Tendrils spread around me, through me. One evil strand brushed my mind, and I screamed.

My hands tensed on the shovel I held until my entire body trembled. The impenetrable blackness rose above me like a slavering beast ready to pounce on its prey. I used the tricks learned over the years of discipline and training to hold it back. Meditation, mantra recitation, denial, acceptance of self, I tried them all.

They failed.

Flashes of vivid light around the darkness offered some small relief. I focused on them, more in desperation than hope. My desolation grew as I stared at a world more like Mars than any I knew. Ditches. Earth torn apart and left open in raw gouges. A grave? Had I blundered into a cemetery? An earthquake? It seemed different from any natural catastrophe, more directed, yet less extensive. Confusion over my new world made me dizzy. Fear caused my heart to race wildly, out of control.

I fell to my knees and stared at the heavens, imploring God to intervene. Prayer did no good. The infinite blackness came hurtling down. I tried to throw the shovel away. Like glue, it stuck to my hands. I lifted it as a defense against the encroaching gloom. My shoulders ached from the strain of holding it so tightly; my mind recoiled from the horror I saw around it, through it.

The ground opened to swallow me, and the black fog descended to wrap me in its suffocating embrace. Choking, I tried to fight. My chest collapsed under invisible weight. My nose and mouth filled with cottony mist. Worst of all, my senses vanished.

I became blind and deaf and totally isolated from the world. Death came for me.

The shovel crashed to the floor with a loud, ringing clank. The beclouding haze left me slowly. I felt bruises rising as I fought against the straps. Barbara Chan yelled something. I didn't hear. My head wanted to explode.

She ripped free the leather straps. I ripped at the wires on my arms, forehead and chest. Sucking in a deep breath caused my lungs to explode.

The image of the killing fog returned, and I screamed in abject fear.

"Peter, stop it!" Strong hands gripped my shoulders and shook hard until my teeth rattled. "Stop it. The experiment is over. The equipment is turned off. You're not being shocked anymore."

"Can't you calm him?" came Michaelson's annoyed question. "If you can't, I can get a resident to give him a sedative."

I kept my eyes screwed shut. To open them meant I had to look at the death plunging down on top of me, crushing me flat, entombing me for all eternity.

"Peter, it's Barbara. Do you know where you are?"

"He's faking," said Michaelson. "There was nothing on the strip recorder to show any change in his galvanic skin response. I got nothing on the EEG or the other monitors. There's not a chance that the equipment malfunctioned and shocked him. This is just an act, Barbara. I'm not sure if I am going to approve this for your thesis topic."

Barbara's strong hands left my shoulders. I slipped from the chair and huddled on the cold floor, feeling the dubious safety and comfort of a wall behind me. The fetal position strained my back and legs, but I couldn't unwind. My fear of the intense, devouring blackness persisted.

"Dr. Michaelson, something happened. That ought to be enough to convince you this is a legitimate area for research."

"He's a fraud," the physicist said bitterly. "You shouldn't waste your time on this. This experiment goes a long ways toward showing that."

"I saw the readouts, Doctor," Barbara Chan said. "There didn't seem to be any significant metabolic change, but we're talking about mental results. Nonlinear changes we might not be able to detect. Something frightened him. *Look* at him."

David Michaelson snorted in contempt. "He's a performer, and you're his audience. I refuse to believe this is anything but an act. There were no physiological changes recorded. His heart rate even slowed. When we go over the videotape, you'll believe me."

"Videotape?" I asked weakly. Stretching my cramped muscles sent new waves of pain through my body, but this was preferable to the psychic fear that had seized me so completely.

"Our stage magician returns to the world of the living," Michaelson said sarcastically. "We videotaped everything. I've got your facial expressions on tape. Once we correlate it with voice stress and the physical responses, we'll have enough to show that you weren't receiving any psychometric signals from the tool but were performing."

"Performing?" I shook my head and regretted it. A black widow spider had spun its web in my brain. I felt both the feathery strands of its web and the dripping venom from its fangs as it ate the inside of my skull. Forcing away the unpleasant sensation, I stood up and rubbed my bare chest. The saline paste Barbara Chan had used to attach the electrodes rubbed off as I scratched. I smiled weakly at the graduate assistant when she used a damp rag to wipe away the paste on my forehead. I remembered what she had said earlier about this being sexy for her. It was anything but that for me, even if she was strikingly beautiful.

Barbara Chan hardly looked the part of fledgling physicist. I have seen less attractive women making a living as models. From the brief talk I had with her before agreeing to this preliminary experiment, I had learned she was also an accomplished actress and sometimes got parts in dinner theatre productions. I had appreciated her tall, svelte loveliness too much. Putting myself in the role of a guinea pig was dangerous.

"Performance," declared Michaelson. "That's all it was. He is putting on an act for our benefit. He can't do any of the stunts he claims."

"Dr. Michaelson, what do I have to gain by coming here?" I asked. The question took him aback. It gave me a chance to collect my own wits. The threat of the black cloud descending over me and squashing my straining body still flustered me. I took the rag from Barbara Chan and finished the simple ablutions.

"You want notoriety. You want a cachet of scientific approval. You think you can gain recognition through me. You're enough of an egotist to think you can dupe me."

"Barbara approached me, not the other way around,"

I pointed out. "I agreed to the experiments because I am curious about my abilities. *I* want to find out how I psychometrize."

"There's no such thing," scoffed Michaelson. "If I had the time, I'd show how you faked all this."

I said nothing. I had read about him in *Who's Who in American Science* and had inquired about his credentials before agreeing to this test by his graduate assistant. No one had mentioned he was one of "them"—a professional debunker. They can chase after the men and women who track flying saucers and ride to Zeta Reticuli and believe the Earth is flat and hollow and filled with Nazis all they want. Most claims of that type are harmless and not to be taken seriously.

There is nothing faked about my skill. Choosing the proper mode of relaxation allows me to separate body from soul. It is my soul, my spirit or essence or whatever term might apply, that studies objects projected onto an astral plane. I psychometrize. Resonance from the object fills me and I "see" with more than my eyes. Strong psychic events influence inanimate objects. This gives a decipherable imprint, inadequate most times, precise at others. The force of the mind making the psychic impression is more important than any other factor.

Some items, such as those of a personal nature, also lie within my realm, though they require a different, lighter form of meditation to read. The proximity and duration of contact is the determining factor in such readings. A valued piece of jewelry, such as a wedding ring, reveals much about its wearer. I once determined that a simple gold ring had been stolen because its imprint differed dramatically from the aura of the woman wearing it. When confronted, the woman wearing it broke down and confessed that she had stolen the ring.

Deeper probing showed the woman's lack of self-esteem, her need to show the world she had married when in fact she had not, and her desperate desire for acceptance. My recommendation for psychiatric counselling resulted in a better person—and the owner of the ring regained her treasured property.

I shuddered as I glanced across the hospital emergency

room at the shovel I had dropped. Prodigious psychic power had imprinted the tool. The only source of that much energy was death. Whoever had held the shovel had died horribly. Even though it wasn't cold in the emergency room, I shivered.

"He's got marvelous body control. You have to admit that," said Michaelson.

"Yes, Doctor," Barbara Chan said.

I stared at her. The woman's tone indicated she found me as attractive as I did her. I damned myself for letting her unduly influence me into agreeing to this experiment. She looked to be in her mid-twenties. I was only thirty-one and in excellent physical condition.

It was a shame I had let physical attraction obliterate good sense.

"He's a stage magician, Barbara," Michaelson said in exasperation. "He earns his money by duping others. Sleight-of-hand. Magic."

"Sleight-of-hand," I agreed. "I might call it magic, but what I do as a stage performer is mostly misdirection. That does not mean I lack the psychometric abilities you were trying to measure."

"Please," Barbara said, forestalling further argument. "I've been over the interview you gave me a dozen times." Her dark, almond-shaped eyes gleamed. "I'm convinced there is a significant thesis here, but I need more information. For instance, you never said how you came by your ability."

"It wasn't pleasant," I said, not wanting to relive that terrifying moment of my life. The woman seemed sincere, and I had agreed to cooperate. Perhaps telling the story once more would shed light on how I am able to read inanimate objects. If nothing else, it would take my mind away from the psychic imprint on the shovel.

"Please," she urged.

I sat on the chair and pulled on my shirt. The silk felt cool next to my skin. I shivered again. The shovel still bothered me unduly, even though it lay far from me. Something had concentrated a man's entire psychic force into that simple rusty tool.

"I used to do an escape act. Some of the most

complicated-appearing escapes are really quite easy. As is usually the case, the ones that seem the simplest are the most deadly. Houdini's milk-can escape is one of those.''

"I remember that one," Barbara said. "You're chained and put into a large metal milk can upside down. The can is filled with water.''

I nodded. "The escape is not only from the strait jacket but from the water-filled can. It requires the ability to dislocate one or both shoulders and the lung capacity for holding your breath a minimum of three minutes.''

"Skilled athletes can do that," interrupted Michaelson.

"True. I work hard to keep in shape for such escapes. This time, though, one buckle jammed. I spent almost four minutes freeing myself from the straight jacket. Escaping the can itself would have taken another two minutes.''

I took a deep, calming breath as I remembered my struggles and how it had become increasingly obvious to me that I would not get free before drowning.

"Your assistants had to get you free?" Barbara leaned forward, hands on her knees, a rapt expression on her face.

"They did. They rushed me to the hospital. Blood vessels had burst in both lungs and in my brain. A tiny section of my cerebellum was destroyed—or activated. After I was discharged from the hospital, I found that I could touch objects and get an extraordinary mental picture of the person owning them.''

"The shovel," asked Barbara, almost breathlessly, "was a control object. It has no history. I found it in the janitor's closet. What did you see when you held it?''

Putting sensations I receive from an object into words is difficult. I tried and failed. Shaking my head, I said, "There was death in everything I saw. The dark cloud coming down, the crushing weight on my chest; those strongly indicate a man was killed while holding the shovel.''

"Bullshit," grumbled Michaelson. "It's just a shovel. Nothing like that has imprinted the metal. You wanted to put on a performance for us and nothing more.''

"Believe what you will," I said. I was too tired to argue. He would never approve Barbara's work, so I had nothing to lose being curt with him.

"What other abilities do you possess, Peter?" Barbara asked.

"What do you mean?" The question startled me.

"Can you move objects with your mind? Psycho-kinesis?"

"That's action at a distance," I scoffed. "That's not possible. It violates the laws of physics."

"Can you predict the future? Read minds?"

"No," I said, not liking Barbara's line of inquiry. "I pick up psychic vibrations. I do this by transporting myself to an astral plane. I don't cast horoscopes—or even believe in astrology. I don't dance under the full moon and smear chicken fat over my naked body, either."

"A pity," she said, a smile creeping up to the corners of her lips. I didn't know what she was getting at. Then my own smile matched hers. There is a matching reso-nance when I touch a psychically imprinted object, just as there is a resonance when one person talks to another and the chemistry is right. Barbara Chan's wavelength was coming closer and closer to matching mine. It had more to do with physical rather than psychic power on our part, but then that was what had brought me here in the first place.

"That's enough," Michaelson said abruptly. "Check the videotapes, Barbara. Give me a full workup. Run the data we collected through the computer. I want to know every muscle twitch and how it correlates to the videos. Then I want you to report everything to me."

"Of course, Dr. Michaelson," she said, rising grace-fully and going to the equipment. Michaelson shot me a look usually reserved for drivers cutting you off during rush hour, then left the emergency room.

"I'm sorry it worked out like this, Peter," Barbara said. "We blew every last circuit in our lab. I thought the med school's emergency room would be all right. They had most of the monitoring equipment here and ready." I watched her with some appreciation. Even the stark white lab coat she wore couldn't hide her trim figure.

"The locale wasn't responsible," I said, looking back

at the blood stains on the wall. What had been the outcome of *that* disaster? "I can't control it at all. Images
force themselves on me. At other times, I get nothing."

"Why not?"

"Sometimes I am too tired. At others, there isn't a
strong enough imprint on the object. And others—I just
don't know. I volunteered for this experiment to learn,
also."

Barbara straightened and ran her hand through her long
black hair. "I'm afraid we didn't get anything important.
It's as if we were running a baseline. There's no significant
deviation from your rest state."

"I go into a trance," I said. "Call it astral projection,
if you like, when my spirit withdraws from my body. There
might not be any physiological changes."

"You said your heart beat rapidly when you saw the
black cloud," Barbara pointed out. "I double checked
that portion of our strip chart recording. Your heart never
varied from its fifty-eight beats per minute."

"My psychic heart sped up," I corrected. "My physical one was left behind in my body."

"That seems odd to me," she said, obviously doubting
me. I watched the clouds forming as she worked hard to
convince herself that her advisor was right and that she
was wasting her time.

"May I?" I took Barbara's calculator from the small
carrying pouch where she slung it at her waist. I held it
for several seconds, settling my mind and lowering myself
into the proper mental state. There are dozens of focal
points to achieve such a meditative state. This time I pictured myself floating like a feather among white, fluffy
clouds. The winds carried me aloft and I relaxed, the earth
below out of sight. Infinite blue stretched above me, beck-
oned and drew and soothed. I didn't try for deep images.
I was content to skim the surface and take whatever slight
imprint message there was to find.

Tiny flashes of Barbara Chan's life came to me. She had
used this calculator for over six years.

"A gift," I said, not sure if I spoke with a physical or
psychic voice. "From your parents. You graduated from

Berkeley. I recognize buildings. Sather Gate. Your classes in Le Conte Hall . . .''

"I was a physics major," she said softly. Her voice took on a steely edge. "Of course I took classes there and in Birge Hall."

The words echoed from afar. She spoke and shared the same room—yet we were separated by more than distance. I had left my body and saw only the colorful, shifting images emanating from the calculator. It was like watching a poorly edited music video blending speech fragments and images in a haphazard pattern.

"Strawberry Creek," I continued. "The Eucalyptus Grove with . . . his name is Greg. You and he—"

I put down the calculator and crashed back into my body. Sweat beaded on my forehead and I felt like a Peeping Tom. Barbara Chan had taken her calculator with her everywhere because of its utility and because it had been given her by her deceased parents. Barbara and her boyfriend had been intimate while students walked by not ten feet from them, and I had witnessed it.

"You couldn't have known," she said, pale.

"Not everything," I said. "I'm sorry. I didn't mean to pry, but it was the strongest impression from the calculator. Do you love him?"

"I haven't seen him in two years. He graduated and married an English major," the woman said with some bitterness. It didn't take a psychometrician or a telepath to realize Greg had meant a great deal to her, and she felt betrayed by him.

"Can we try again?" Barbara asked.

The question startled me. After all I'd said about her lamented lover, I thought she'd want nothing more to do with psychometry.

"Isn't that up to Dr. Michaelson? If he doesn't approve your research topic, you'd just be wasting your time."

"We can continue. There's nothing conclusive about what we collected tonight. Damn, who's calling?" The graduate student rushed to a gunmetal gray government surplus desk and scooped up the phone. Her expression changed from annoyance to wonder.

"It's for you, Peter. It's the police. You didn't tell them I'd kidnapped you, did you?"

I took the phone from Barbara, our fingers touching briefly. I had run into a friend with SFPD at lunch and mentioned, in passing, that I would be here tonight. I hadn't thought anything about it at the time. Forgetting that a policeman never forgets now robbed me of needed rest. No matter how bone-weary I get, another claim on my time and energy always comes. I hung up after agreeing to meet with Detective Worthington.

"What did the police want?" asked Barbara.

"A murder," I said. "They want me to go over the scene and see what I can find—psychometrize. I've worked with them before."

Tiredly, I finished dressing. A murder on top of being shocked and crushed and tied up would be a fitting end to the night.

CHAPTER TWO

San Francisco isn't a large city with uncontrolled urban sprawl. In some ways it is more of a windup toy of a city than a major metropolitan center like London or Tokyo, but it has charm. The quiet middle-class suburb at the base of the Twin Peaks not far from Golden Gate Park was dotted with restored Victorian houses, complete with Queen Anne lacy gingerbread. The small stuccoed house in the middle of the street ought to have fit right in, with its mid-twenties art deco architecture.

What distinguished it from the other houses on the street were the police lines and flashing red and blue lights. Murder had been committed here.

"Are you sure this is all right?" Barbara Chan asked.

"No one forced you to come," I said. Finding a parking space, even with the police directing traffic, proved difficult. I wheeled my red BMW 521i into a tight space at the end of the street. "You could have stayed in your lab and analyzed the data on me."

"There wasn't anything to analyze, Peter. Your bodily responses were neutral throughout the experiment."

Shivers raced up my spine and caused gooseflesh to ripple on my arms. The sense of being crushed by the enveloping black cloud was too real. I know when my gift—or curse—manifested itself. The questions of how and why might remain unanswered if Dr. Michaelson's attitude didn't change and he let Barbara pursue the investigation into my powers. The physicist had decided that psychometry was impossible. Since it was impossible, I was a fake. QED.

Another researcher with a more open mind might be able to answer the questions I had about myself and my talent—someone like Barbara. A slow smile crept over my lips as I turned and looked at her. She might be just the one to do the proper research. That could be mutually enlightening and enjoyable.

I stopped at the police line. The uniformed officer came over and waved me back, bored with his job. He had seen too many curious sightseers tonight.

"Run along. This is police business," he said. The boredom in his face carried over to his words. He performed perfunctorily. I could be the killer returning to the scene and he would never suspect.

"Detective Worthington called me."

"It was arranged," cut in Barbara, still nervous at being involved in a police investigation. "The sergeant in charge asked for Mr. Thorne."

The policeman looked from me to Barbara and back, reluctantly. He frowned.

"What's the name again?" The uniformed officer's apathy changed subtly. Anyone asked in on a case by a detective sergeant might be worth being polite to.

I introduced myself and more formally gave particulars on Barbara.

"Oh, you must be part of the forensics team. Why didn't you just show your ID?" He held up the yellow plastic POLICE BARRICADE ribbon and let us slip under it. I knew he watched Barbara more than he did me. Misdirection. The key to stage magic.

I walked off before Barbara could tell the officer we weren't with the medical examiner's office or assigned to a forensics unit. She hurried along behind me, through the small entryway and down the corridor littered with dozens of potted plants. I recognized a few of the varieties. At the end of the entryway a large red-flowering bougainvillaea dominated an entire wall. From here we turned up a cramped flight of steps and went into the house.

Willie Worthington stood to one side of the living room, staring at his notebook as if the murderer's name might appear by magic on the page. He had often asked me about automatic writing and how spirits guide a human hand. I doubted Worthington believed in spirits; at times I wasn't sure he believed in psychometry, although I had given him valuable information in the past.

"Peter, glad you made it so fast. I've chased the vultures out."

"You're letting me in before the forensics team? I'm flattered," I said, meaning it. The forensics squads are highly trained, but after they finish with a murder scene, the psychic resonance is often ruined. They photograph and dust and take items for tests beyond my comprehension. When they are done, their modern scientific methods have reduced the resonance I sense to vague echoes.

"I said I chased them off, not kept them out. Who's this?" Worthington asked, pointing his pencil at Barbara. "Another one of the psychic sniffers? If so, they're getting better-looking all the time. Might not bother calling you next time."

Barbara smiled sweetly. I knew Willie Worthington too well to think it had any real effect on him. She said, "I'm a friend of Peter's."

"Some people have all the luck. Me, I get all the headaches." Worthington chewed vigorously on his pencil. He waited for me to finish the introduction.

"She's a grad student at San Francisco University," I said. "A physicist and researcher interested in psychic phenomena."

"Physics type, huh?" Worthington said. He chewed at the eraser end of his pencil. Teeth marks halfway down the pencil showed that he never bothered erasing. The rubber end had long since been removed by his beaverlike gnawing. "You do NMR work?"

Barbara's eyes widened in surprise. "I have done low-temperature nuclear magnetic resonance research. How did you know?"

"That's why you and Peter got together, right? He's all the time talking about sensing resonance in the stuff he picks up. Hmm." Worthington turned away and flipped to a new page. What he entered was beyond guessing.

"You deduced that?" Barbara pressed.

"Hell, no. I was nosing around the school a while back and saw you in a lab. Science stuff interests me." Worthington hitched up his sagging pants and chomped down on his pencil. These were signs that the polite preliminaries were over and he was ready to talk about the crime.

A slow circuit of the room gave me a picture of the people who lived here. A couple, no children, or children grown and moved away. The lack of pictures of any offspring probably meant no children. Even empty-nesters have mementos of children around, marriages, graduations, service or school photos, grandchildren's snapshots.

The woman kept house full time. The only dust in the room was well hidden from prying eyes. The casual litter indicated no visitors had called recently. Such a meticulous woman would have been sure to pick up a pair of discarded magazines before anyone had dropped in. The furniture was old but sturdy and, at one time, expensive. It was out of date now, but the loving care lavished on polishing it and taking care of the occasional nicks on the oak legs showed it had moved into heirloom class.

"There's no sign of a struggle," I said. "Is the body in there?" I indicated a short hall that probably led to a bedroom.

"She's back there," said Worthington. "It's not as bad as some of them, but unless you're used to it . . ." He eyed Barbara, subtly warning her she was going to lose supper unless she had viewed dead bodies before. Worthington had called me on four prior cases. None had been especially bloody, at least from the way the police talked about other cases, but I'd had trouble eating for days afterward, and sleep had been troubled after each one.

I had learned to take the time to meditate and control my overly zealous imagination. The quiet and contemplation had aided me in distancing myself from the victim. I could feel for them but did not have to assume the guilt for their deaths.

"How was she killed?" I asked.

"Two gunshots, from the back. The bullets were crudely cut into dumdums. They spread fast in her brain and blew away most of her face when they came out. We're going on the assumption she's the woman who lived here. Both her teeth and her face are an unholy mess." Worthington shifted sideways and got his bulky belly past another officer, then ambled down the hallway, his broad shoulders brushing the walls on either side.

"You don't have to look," I told Barbara. "This might

be much worse than other cases I've been associated with.''

"I want to see you work," Barbara said. "Detective Worthington sounds like a pragmatic person. I want to see how you help—even more than his forensics technicians.''

I shrugged. She'd learn how messy a murder can be. It might be good for her education, though I felt strangely protective. I squeezed past Worthington and into the victim's bedroom. She was dressed for bed in a peach-colored nylon negligee. It wasn't anything expensive, but neither was it cheap. The victim had had good tastes, in decorating and in clothing.

"Don't move her," Worthington said, pointing at the face-down corpse. "We've got the photographers working over the rest of the house. You've got five minutes, ten at the outside, Peter, before I let them loose to finish here.''

"I appreciate your confidence, Willie.''

"This one might be impossible without you.''

"Why?'' I asked, surprised. The crime seemed straightforward. Then I began thinking. There weren't any signs of forced entry. Looking around the bedroom didn't show any disturbance of the orderly dressers. The jewelry chest drawers were all closed. I got no sense of robbery anywhere. "I see,'' I said slowly. "A motiveless crime.''

"She wasn't raped, she wasn't robbed. There might have been an open door downstairs, leading to the garage. We're checking on that. And the killer left that behind.'' Worthington pointed to an old Army-issue .45 automatic.

"I need to touch it.''

"Go ahead. I looked it over so hard my eye tracks are on it. No fingerprints.''

"You can't be sure,'' blurted Barbara. "You need special chemicals. An epoxy vapor deposition test will bring out prints you can't see.''

"It's part of the pattern, Doc,'' he said. "There won't be any prints. The killer was damned efficient.'' He stared at Barbara and added, "Besides all that, I put the damned thing into a plastic bag. Nobody's going to get fingerprints on it that aren't there already.''

Barbara started to argue. Worthington moved farther into the room and let her see the body. From the back, the holes were hardly the size of my index finger. The victim lay half-across the bed. Blood puddled beneath her destroyed face. Forcing down my rising gorge, I sucked in slow, deep breaths to cleanse both body and soul. The aura, the vitality that had been this woman, had long since faded. The flesh does not retain the resonance I sense for more than a few seconds after death.

I hunkered down by the automatic. The U.S. Army had purchased millions of the weapons since its initial issue in 1911. Pawn shops across the country were filled with them. Reaching out, I placed my hands just above the weapon in its plastic bag. Heat boiled up and threatened to burn my flesh.

I settled my mind and experienced the strange disconnection of body and soul needed for psychometry. The energy radiating from the weapon was strong, very strong.

Trembling, I placed my hands on the metal. The plastic barrier did nothing to hold back the waves of hatred I felt.

Into the room, filled with anger and hurt. Kill. Kill the bitch! Kill the fallen angel! Pluck her wings! Quiet, be quiet, don't disturb her, in the bath like I thought.

She's coming out. Steady, steady, do it. You slut! You stinking slut! Fallen angel!

I fell backward and crashed into the wall. My heart rhythm turned erratic as I moved away from the pistol. Sweat poured down my face. I held out my hands and saw how they trembled. Looking up, I saw Worthington chewing on his pencil and Barbara wanting to come to my aid but not knowing if she should.

"I saw him. I felt him do it. The way the automatic bucked in his hand. The . . . the sheer glee he took killing her was terrible!"

"Who was it, Peter?" Worthington asked gently.

"Medium height, five ten or so. Weight around two hundred. A scar on his right thumb. I saw it as I looked down when I—he—cocked the automatic. The hatred inside me, him." I took a deep breath and distanced myself from the image still lingering in my head. "Her husband killed her," I said with conviction. No question existed about his identity.

"We've got problems with that. Her husband is in L.A.

on business, at an auto trade show, and has been for two days."

"He did it," I said positively. "He thought his wife was having an affair. I don't know with whom. He planned this for months. It's been festering inside him, growing like a cancer until it took control of him. There's some sort of religious fervor attached. He kept thinking of her as a fallen angel."

"We don't know much about him. Might be a religious freak. There's plenty of them around these days willing to cut your throat for your own good." Worthington chewed until yellow flakes of paint from his pencil dotted his lips.

"He bought the pistol somewhere else. I caught a flash of neon lights." I tried hard to get the harsh emotions into a far corner of my mind by concentrating on other images I had received.

"A pawn shop?"

"Reno, Las Vegas, somewhere like that," I said. "He thought it was appropriate getting the gun where there were other fallen angels and sinners." I hadn't realized so much information had come to me until Worthington asked and I began analyzing my impressions. The information from the Colt automatic had flooded me, drowned me under the searing hatred. "He's had the pistol for weeks."

"He was in L.A. this afternoon. He's out partying with a hundred businessmen. The details aren't clear, but it looks like they're out getting their rocks off at a strip joint." Worthington snorted in disgust and shook his head as if such behavior was incomprehensible.

"He did it," I repeated.

"That's only a guess," said Barbara. "You know it wasn't a burglar or valuables would have been taken. And there wasn't any sign of a break-in, right?"

Worthington ignored her. The detective curled his lip and held his pencil under his nose, then snatched it away and wrote frantically in his notebook.

"The airport," I said. "He took a commuter flight up, then back. How long has it been since she was killed?"

"The ME didn't like me chasing him out before he did a complete workup, but from a neighbor's testimony, not long. One old geezer across the street's got insomnia, he says. He was staring out the window, didn't see any lights over here, but he did hear a shot about two hours back.''

"Did he hear the second one, also?"

"He can't be sure. He's a bit hard of hearing. He might have missed the first and heard the second. If that's what happened, the shots were several seconds apart. He got worried and called us. We were here within ten minutes.''

"I can't tell how far apart the shots were," I admitted. Time flows strangely as I hold objects and psychometrize them. Emotional imprinting gives the resonance I interpret, not the passage of time. Events are fixed by what the person feels rather than what a clock reports.

"He's on a commuter flight," I said. "Have police in L.A. waiting. He'll be on one."

Worthington motioned to the other detective who had entered the room and stood around, looking amused at everything I said. Worthington's signal sent him scampering from the room.

"It's worth a try," the detective said. "You get any more out of the murder weapon?"

I looked at it, then at the dead woman. I shook my head. There was something pitiful about this case. There was so little, and I felt there should have been more. A life had been taken. California divorce laws are liberal. If the man had truly believed his wife was having an affair, he could have gotten a divorce. He didn't have to kill her.

And yet he did—and in some way, he *had* to murder her. I'd shared his overwhelming hatred of his wife and a religious fever that burned without ending.

"She was a harridan," said Worthington. "That's what the neighbors all said. Ruled her husband with an iron hand—no velvet glove for her."

"That's not reason enough to kill her!" protested Barbara. On this point we agreed.

"I need to let the forensics team back in. They're about ready to chew up the carpets by now, unless I miss my guess." Worthington yelled down the hall, "Get your stuff in here and do a complete workup. We got a suspect. Now prove he's the one who did it."

Worthington smiled crookedly and said to me, "Keeps

'em on their feet if they think I know who did it and they don't."

"It must look good in your report, too," said Barbara. She still seemed shocked from viewing the murder victim.

"Yeah, Doc, it does," Worthington said dryly. "You two want a cup of coffee? I got some time to kill while those yahoos wave their magic wands and do their chants."

"Excuse me," Barbara cut in. "Detective Worthington, you're saying a scientific team is performing magical acts and yet you just watched Peter psychometrize—"

"Magic, science, what's the difference? It's all just names. Let's get the coffee. Burnside, we'll be down the street at the Doggie Diner."

"Not again, Sarge," the other detective complained. "I don't want to put up with your belly ache if you eat another dozen of their hot dogs."

"It's the coffee that gets to me," Worthington said, parking his pencil behind his ear. He motioned to us to follow him down the narrow stairs and past the small gauntlet of greenery and into the night. Wind whipped off the Bay and turned the night chilly. Remembering the ordeal I had been through made it all the colder.

Barbara had asked if I used my psychometric powers during my nightclub act. I'd said no. The reason, other than the psychic drain, was the long-term emotional toll it took on me. I couldn't get the stark, sordid, searing hate of the woman's husband out of my mind. And when I did, the memory of the blackness crushing down on me returned. I would live with these two psychometric readings for a long, long time.

We walked in silence until we got to the giant plastic dog's head that dominated the corner. Worthington went inside, no stranger to food causing intense gastric distress in lesser mortals. He only ordered three of the hot dogs. I settled for a Coke, never having learned to like either the smell or taste of coffee. Barbara ordered coffee, took a sip and made a face. She laced it with enough sugar to give a diabetic an attack, then added a healthy dollop of the synthetic creamer. She still made faces as she drank it.

"Let's sit and talk over there," said Worthington,

around a mouthful of hot dog. "You know, these tax my powers as a detective."

"What?" asked Barbara.

"Mystery meat. You never know what they put into hot dogs." Worthington stuffed the rest of his first into his mouth, munched and then attacked the second.

"You've done good work for me, Peter. I appreciate it. The soda's on me. Your coffee's on me, too, Doc," he said, pointing a mustard-stained finger in the direction of Barbara's coffee.

"You keep calling me 'Doc.' I don't have my Ph.D. yet." Barbara seemed amused at Worthington. She had no idea how sharp the man was when it came to solving a crime.

"Doesn't matter. All you college types qualify, in my book." He finished the hot dog in two more gulps. "We figured it might be the husband. Peter's work gives us something to go on, something we only guessed at. If he's really been partying hearty down in L.A., who's to know if he skipped out for a few hours? His friends will be drunk and swear to anything. And he wouldn't have any trouble finding a dozen new friends to say he was with them. That's the way big conventions are. He's some kind of car dealer. You know how they are." Worthington licked the relish from his fingers and belched. When he had cleared the gas, he began gobbling the last hot dog.

"Can you be so sure? Who else could it be?" demanded Barbara.

"This is a wacky world, Doc. We got people going around and killing for no reason." Worthington looked around and said in a lower voice, "That's why we called in Peter. I had a gut feeling this might be the start of another serial killing. Fits the pattern of a set back in Detroit. You don't hear me saying this too often, but I'm damned glad I was wrong."

I shuddered. Dealing with a serial killer was nothing I looked forward to. Willie Worthington had not called me in on what turned out to be a routine case simply to get out of doing some elementary police work. He had wanted to establish quickly that this was not the work of a mad dog killer.

Worthington's beeper sounded. "Be right back," he said, sliding out awkwardly from the table. He spoke rapidly into the pay telephone at the end of the stained plastic counter for several minutes, then hung up. He returned with a broad smile on his face.

"A good night's work. A man answering to the description Peter gave us was apprehended getting off the commuter flight into LAX. The two cops taking him into custody could barely Mirandize him before he started spewing out the most God-awful filth you ever heard."

"About his wife?"

"Called her a slut, a fallen angel, and a lot worse." Worthington looked at me significantly. "Those were his *exact* words. He confessed three times on the way to the precinct station. Yes, this is one good night's work." Worthington belched and left the diner.

I just stared at Barbara across the table. Her gaze met mine, but the thoughts behind those dark eyes were unreadable. She had believed, and yet she hadn't, before this. Her advisor had influenced her thoughts, but the reading I did on her calculator had started her thinking for herself.

This added to the questions burning in her. I saw it, and approved. I wanted to see more of her. But not now, even though I saw she'd spend the night with me if I asked. For my part, I had to go home and try to elude the cruel thoughts still lingering from my work.

CHAPTER THREE

Blackness, intense, impenetrable, falling, falling, crushing me to death.

I awoke from the dream, panting and drenched in sweat. Getting out of bed, I paced back and forth for several minutes until it became apparent this wasn't going to help me drive away the evil images from Barbara Chan's experiment. I had finally come to grips with the image of the man murdering his wife. The experiment with the shovel still gnawed at my mind.

I tried to determine why. The answer came slowly. A man had killed his wife, and I had coped with this type of upsetting psychometric impression before. The shovel holder had died; I had died with him. It worked at that part of me—of everyone—that fears death.

Opening the sliding glass door in the living room let in a wet, bracing breeze from across the Bay. I shivered, then stepped out onto the small balcony, naked and reveling in the stimulation the moist, cool air gave me.

From my aerie, there were few who might see me and complain. I had an unobstructed view of the Golden Gate Bridge in one direction, and by leaning out precariously, I could see Coit Tower to the east. Eyes closed and body still reacting to the impressions of crushing death I had received from the shovel, I tried to relax.

Meditation had not worked before I turned in for the night. The emotional impact of the self-righteously murderous husband had kept me from the level of concentration required then. Some of those ghosts had been exorcised by two hours of reading. I had finished a stack of news magazines and gone on to a horror novel. Something about the novel's young hero soothed me. He was beset by a personal fiend masquerading as a phantom pet that sometimes killed and sometimes aided him. At the end of the book, he had come to grips with the destructiveness inherent in this relationship.

I saw parallels with my own talent—or curse. It could destroy as easily as it could save. I had helped bring to justice a murderer tonight but felt no sense of accomplishment. The man who had held the shovel had died horribly. I was sure of it. And the force of *that* image harried me.

It had to be harnessed, just as the protagonist of the horror novel had dealt with his personal demon.

Looking toward Coit Tower, I was surprised to see the rays of sunlight poking above the Berkeley Hills far behind it. I had read until almost four and had drifted off for less than an hour before coming out here. Daylight had crept up on me while I endlessly went over my plaguing impressions from Barbara's experiment.

San Francisco stirred and would soon come completely alive. I went inside and found a robe, pulling it around me and returning to the balcony. The pungent smell of toast and coffee rose from the apartment below. My nose wrinkled and I turned away involuntarily. Toast was fine. The coffee aroma caused my stomach to churn. I tried to ignore it and watch the sunrise. Failing this, I went inside and poured out a bowl of Apple Cinnamon Squares. I didn't bother adding milk. I ate them dry and enjoyed the crunch.

The ringing phone stopped me halfway back to the balcony. I hesitated to answer it. My mood had not lightened, sleep had eluded me all night long, and I did not want to deal with ordinary nuisances. Against my better judgment, I swallowed the mouthful of wheat and fruit and picked up the phone.

"What do you want?" I made no pretense at sounding friendly. Anyone calling me early in the morning got what he deserved. That I had missed an entire night's sleep only added to my grumpiness.

"Peter?" The voice sounded familiar, but I couldn't put a face to it.

"Yes."

"This is Barbara, Barbara Chan." My mood lightened a little. This didn't keep me from stifling a loud yawn. "I'm not disturbing you, am I?"

"It's been a hard night," I said, not wanting to itemize all the problems I'd had since I had dropped her off at her Oakland apartment.

"I wanted to check on you, to see how you were doing. You seemed pretty . . . frazzled last night."

"Is that a physics term, 'frazzled'?"

She laughed and I felt better by the minute. "I've been talking with Dr. Michaelson."

"You told him what happened?" There was a long pause. Barbara was trying to phrase her advisor's reply in terms less abrasive than he was likely to have used.

"Yeah," she said. "He thought it was all just simple observation on your part. He did everything but call me a liar and Detective Worthington a fool. I even heard him mumble 'Clever Hans' as I left his office."

"Sorry you won't be able to continue the experiment. I *did* want to learn what's really behind my talent." Surprisingly, I was sorry the experiment was at an end. Seeing Barbara again might be more difficult, especially since her advisor had taken such a dislike to me.

"What makes you think I'm giving up so easily?" she asked. "My lot in life should not be to defend my advisor professor. I'm his graduate assistant, not his slave."

"He can ruin your career," I pointed out.

"He's an asshole, but not that big a one," Barbara said.

I wasn't so sure. I had seen too many men with closed minds to doubt their cruelty and outright maliciousness when crossed. Again, she surprised me with her sudden question.

"Is it possible to learn to become a psychometrician without sustaining brain damage?"

This made me pause for a moment. I had never considered the matter before. Resonance from inanimate objects invaded my brain and caused the images I "saw" on the astral plane. Learning how to "see" without a brush with death from a brain hemorrhage might be possible. The only other psychometrician I had ever met who truly had the talent had been born with it, a result of an overeager obstetrician's clumsy use of forceps during birth. But to develop the talent? I had no idea if it was possible.

"This requires some thought on my part," I said.

"I want to try. Dr. Michaelson might not believe what happened during the experiment and later at the murder scene was real, but I spoke with Detective Worthington again."

"What did he say?" I was impressed that she had followed up on what happened last night. I was also curious about Willie Worthington's evaluation of me.

"He was cautiously optimistic about your abilities," she said. "He never once mentioned psychometry, yet gave the impression that was how you worked out the murderer. He's a fascinating man." She giggled. "And he's kind of cute, too."

"Worthington? Cute? He's more complex than he looks. On the outside he's nothing more than an overweight, nervous bureaucrat who's watched too many 'Columbo' reruns. His memory is phenomenal, his knowledge is encyclopedic, and he can put together odd facts to come to remarkable conclusions."

Barbara laughed. It reminded me of the sound of silver bells chiming gently and beautifully. "You two ought to form an official mutual admiration society. He was very complimentary of you, too, even if it was all off the record. He told me he'd deny he even knew you if I tried to publish using any of the cases he mentioned."

"You want to try to learn how I perform the psychometry?"

"I do." The eagerness in her voice wasn't feigned.

"Let's get together and discuss how to approach this," I said, only half-convinced that anything might come of it.

"I'll be over in an hour!"

"Wait, not—" I spoke into a dial tone. Sighing, I replaced the phone in its cradle, finished the Apple Cinnamon Squares and dressed. She was prompt. Almost exactly one hour after she hung up on me, Barbara Chan presented herself at my door.

"I hope I'm not being too presumptuous," she said as she came in. She tossed her coat over a rocking chair near the door. I let out a small sigh as she passed by. The perfume she used set my heart racing. Pheromones would interfere with any serious instruction. In a way, I hoped

Barbara wasn't strictly interested in my talent. It would be quite easy to develop more than a passing interest in her.

"Whatever works," I said.

"I did interrupt. You didn't have someone here?" She looked around my apartment. I wondered how she was sizing me up. The decor left something to be desired from a woman's point of view. The colors were more garish than subtle, and my walls were festooned with old posters from the magic greats. Two original lobby posters from Houdini's 1923 national tour formed the centerpiece of my collection. I had one Thurston poster touting his elaborate "Spirit Cabinet" illusion and another from Blackstone, the elder, not the younger. Barbara stopped and looked at them.

"My heroes," I said.

"Your wife doesn't mind you hanging these things? They're so . . . colorful. You need more subtle hues. Oh, I'm sorry, I'm being too judgmental."

"Your prerogative," I said. "My wife doesn't mind these old posters being everywhere in the apartment because I'm not married."

"Oh." The light in her eyes appealed to me. The ages-old game between man and woman continued, and I wanted to be a willing player—again. The memory of my wife's death five years ago still haunted me when other specters weren't more prominent.

"May I get you something to drink?"

"No, nothing," Barbara Chan said. She sat on the edge of the sofa, intent on my every move. "You will help me try to duplicate your feats, won't you?"

"I don't call them feats any more than I call having twenty/twenty vision a feat. And yes, I will try. It had never occurred to me that it might be possible for another to learn without enduring what I have."

"Dr. Michaelson won't approve my research unless I can show him something definitive. If I can duplicate even a small part of what you do, I might be able to get a handle on designing an experiment that will convince him to let me continue," she said, still leaning forward and showing rapt attention. "His real field is—"

"Nuclear magnetic resonance," I supplied.

"Yes, that's why we got together in the first place. He's the only faculty member doing any kind of NMR work. I dabbled at it as an undergraduate, but finally decided that resonances can be more than atomic in nature. Do you understand nonlinear dynamics, chaotic behavior, strange attractors?"

"I might just understand strange attractions," I said. We both laughed. I had only a small acquaintance with the foundations of chaos, but I knew this was an adequate pun. For the moment.

"I don't make claims for my talent. I don't make money from it. When I work in nightclubs as a mentalist and magician, I use only those skills pioneered by them." I pointed to Thurston and the other illustrious men of stage magic lining my living room walls.

"Is it true you started out working as a street performer?"

I smiled as I remembered my younger days. "In Union Square. I never bothered with permits. I ended up roaming Fisherman's Wharf and doing small tricks for the tourists there. They always seemed amazed when I multiplied foam rubber balls in their hands or pulled coins out from their ears."

Starvation had been a step away when I worked the streets, but it had been an exciting life free of the bonds society puts on most of us. I had married, become an escape artist, seen my wife die of cancer, almost died myself—and gained a talent I would gladly trade for a house plant that wouldn't die on me.

The weight of my psychometries came back to bedevil me.

"You look tired, Peter," she said. "Is there anything I can do? Maybe I should come back later. It was a long night for you."

"No, this is fine. I didn't get much sleep." Explaining to Barbara the problems involved with my type of "seeing" did not deter her from wanting to try. She would not be convinced there was a difference between looking at a candle flame and looking into a laser. Without preparation, the laser burns the retina and blinds forever.

Slut! Fallen angel!

I pushed the demented man's murderous cries from my mind. They weren't immediate any longer. They remained as vicious echoes and nothing more. With great deliberation, I mastered them gradually, as I always had before.

"What do I do? I've practiced meditation techniques since I was a child."

"This might be easier than you think," I said, meaning it. "For a shallow impression, I need only touch an object. It doesn't tell me much, though. Sometimes I don't get anything at all. I need to enter a trance state for the most complete psychometrizing. It feels as if my body and spirit separate. I can wander a short distance, and if I am touching something powerfully charged with psychic energy, I 'see' its aura, and align myself with its resonance."

"Do you visualize it as color, such as that mentioned by people taking Kirlian photographs?"

I shook my head. "Describing it as color or even as substance misses the point. There might not be a good description. It flows, it moves, it conforms generally to the outline of the object. And it's like a music video at times. Pictures flash past, distorted, crazy and out of focus at times. Colors become surreal."

"And?" she prodded. "There's more. What is it, Peter?"

"My senses often become jumbled. I hear sights and taste sound. Or I see sound and feel odor. There isn't any way to predict if this will take place. Interpreting it is complex, but I've had years of experience doing it."

"Fascinating," Barbara said. From the way she looked at me, I wasn't sure if she meant my talent or me. I wasn't sure it mattered, either. The more we talked, the more I hoped she meant me.

"And disturbing. It's hard getting some of the resonances out of my mind. The visions I had during your experiment are still with me. Forcefully."

"I don't know what could have caused that," she said. "I just grabbed the first tool I found. The janitor raised hell when he found I had taken it."

"He didn't know anything of its history?"

"Nothing," she said. "To him it was just another shovel—and one he'd have to pay for if it disappeared."

A bird of blackness spreading its wings above me. Hovering, pausing, swooping down on its prey. Killing, crushing, crushing, crushing, *CRUSHING!*

"Peter, are you all right?" Cool fingers stroked my brow. I came back to the present. Barbara knelt in front of me. I started to sweat in reaction to the nearness of death once more.

"It is a strong image to cope with," I said. "Do you still want to try this?"

"Yes," she said, but with some hesitation.

I rose, went to my CD and put on a recording of environmental sounds, soft wind whistling through tall trees followed by water falling. It didn't seem right. I changed it to a Shadowfax album. This fit my mood better than simple white noise.

"Key on this. Relax, use it as a soft focus, drift, drift, ride with the sounds," I said, my voice becoming a monotone. At one point in my career I had considered becoming a stage hypnotist. The lure of sleight-of-hand magic had triumphed, though I remember much of what I had learned about inducing a trance state in others.

"I'm floating," Barbara said in her soft voice.

"Float, rise, rise," I whispered, my voice merging with that of the wind's susurration.

She leaned back on the sofa, began breathing slowly, deeply, entering what doctors would call an alpha state. I closed my eyes and began the relaxation techniques that I used when performing psychometry. Ten minutes passed while I settled myself. Then I began to match the woman's breathing pattern, consciously adapting my own to hers until they became congruent.

The astral plane where I walk during my deepest psychometry opened for me—and because of our breath-link, the door opened partially for Barbara.

She appeared different on this plane, more lovely and ethereal, if that was possible, a small child bubbling with boundless enthusiasm. I turned slowly, trying to find something on the featureless, shifting plane to hold her attention. Many times as I wander this realm there is nothing of interest happening. At others, the surreal dimension is crowded with sights and sounds of confusing patterns and content.

Peter, am I doing this?

Yes.

I never came this far before.

Come with me, come . . .

I tried to lead her and failed. Her control slipped. Excitement robbed her of the tranquility needed to maintain her position on the astral plane—and she had yet to learn to experience the outrageous distortions here and not be thrust back into our more normal, regular-dimensioned world.

Barbara Chan faded as her concentration foundered. I turned to touch her, to hold her for a few seconds longer when the scream deafened me. It hammered at my ears and eyes and tore at the roots of my brain. Trying to stop it proved impossible.

Shafts of white-hot pain drove mercilessly into my head. The concentration I had thought lacking in Barbara Chan and in which I prided myself broke.

I fell out of my chair and sat on the floor of my living room. The reverberations of that hideous, lingering scream still rattled over and over in my head like razors tumbling in a washing machine.

"Peter?" She looked at me, curiosity overpowering her fear. "What was that?"

I had no idea what I had experienced, but it was potent. Doubly so, if an untrained woman had heard it, too.

CHAPTER FOUR

Sleep came in fitful spurts all day. I had chased Barbara away after hearing the hideous screams on the astral plane, pleading complete exhaustion. She had taken one look at my haggard face and had left, promising to come back.

In a way, I wished she had insisted on staying. There are times when I need someone to do nothing more than hold my hand. This was one of them. David Michaelson thought I was a fraud. If he could slip into my head and see the turmoil there, he'd know how wrong he was.

Every time I drifted off to a disturbed sleep, an image rose to prod me into groggy awareness. It varied from the cloaking black cloud to the religious fervor of the murdering car salesman, and overwhelming both images was the scream.

The *scream*. It had been more than sound in the astral world, though this was the easiest way of describing it. I had tasted salt and seen flashes and then become confused as my senses shifted like quicksilver. The sound had turned to an odor more fitting to a charnel house.

The scream had carried the unmistakable message of death with it. All the more horrible, Barbara had experienced it, too. I felt more than a little guilty exposing her to it through my inept tutelage. She could not have entered the astral world fully without my help. I should have protected her more, even if she had seemed oblivious to the ghastly message locked in it.

Sunlight walked slowly across the living room and quietly left as I tossed and turned on the sofa. The ringing telephone brought me up. I hesitated and considered ignoring it.

The telephone company has built their machines too well. The frequency grated exquisitely on my ears and forced me to answer. I promised myself I'd replace it with a soft chime. But then, I'd made this promise to myself a dozen times before and had always put it off.

"Thorne, how're you doing?"

I recognized Willie Worthington's voice even before the muffled belch cinched the identification.

"Don't eat hot dogs," I said.

"Everyone's a critic. I wanted to call to thank you for your help last night." Worthington paused, then added, "You doing all right? You were a bit shaky."

"What can I do for you?"

Worthington became all business. He cleared his throat and I mentally pictured him opening his spiral notebook to the first page and beginning to read.

"Nasty murder this time, Peter."

"I'm not interested," I said, cutting him off. I needed time alone to put my mental house in order. Even thinking of another crime made me break out in a cold sweat.

"You sure you're okay? You sound like homemade shit."

"I feel like it."

"Sorry I called. I just thought you might be interested in this one since it has all sorts of New Age trimmings to it."

"How's that?" I cursed myself for asking before common sense prevailed.

"Happened this morning out in Marin. A really classy type got it with a crystal knife. Quartz, the report says. Preliminary workup says it's something used in New Age rituals. You'd know more about that than I would."

"I doubt it," I said, turning tired once more. My adrenaline had flowed for a moment. "I appreciate much of the New Age philosophy, but a lot of it is mumbo-jumbo. Channelling is a rip-off, for instance."

"Yeah, it's like that button I saw. Just because you're dead doesn't mean you're smart. It's all claptrap and fakery."

I was vaguely pleased he agreed. Mostly, I just wanted Worthington to let me be miserable.

"She's a looker, isn't she?"

"Who?" I found myself buffeted by Worthington's quick changes of subject.

"Doc. You remember her? The lady you were squiring around last night?"

I remembered that Barbara had spoken with Worthington since then. He was fishing for information. I doubted he meant anything by it. Worthington asked questions just as surely as people breathed to stay alive.

"We might be working together," I said cautiously. "It depends on research money and her advisor's approval."

"How long have you two been hanging out together? She's not like your usual groupie. The doc's a lot classier."

"She's no fan," I said. "Not like you mean." Again common sense failed me. I wanted to divert Worthington from Barbara. For some reason, I wasn't comfortable discussing my attraction to her with the detective. I asked, "When did the murder take place?" I had the queasy feeling that I already knew the answer.

The scream almost deafened me as I remembered its intensity.

"A bit past ten this morning."

I became lost in the ululation of the sound—the feeling—I'd heard on the astral plane. The shriek had been the result of someone dying. Or the death caused the psychic screech. Cause and effect became confused, not only in psychic matters but at the quantum level.

"You still there, Peter?"

"Sorry," I said. "Where exactly was the murder?"

"That's one reason I called to see if you would be interested. It's out of my jurisdiction over in northern Marin County."

"Why are you interested in someone else's case? Don't you have enough to keep you busy?"

Willie Worthington laughed harshly. "I got two new ones this morning. Both look to be easy. One's a drug-related killing. The perp in the other is going to break down and confess any time now. We got men with rubber hoses working on him."

Worthington's sense of humor bothered me at times. He didn't have anyone torturing his suspect, but to joke about mistreatment showed that the idea wasn't far from his mind.

"We're going to get really tough on him at lunch. I'm force feeding him hot dogs."

That took the edge off the matter.

"You want me to look into the Marin killing as a favor to you?"

"Hell, no. I don't care squat about what happens up there. I just thought you might be interested since it does have all that New Age crap involved."

"And?"

"And if you just happen to come across anything having to do with a drug link to a guy named Steve Hackett, you might buy me lunch and let me know."

I swallowed and closed my eyes. Getting involved in another murder this soon after my other psychic upsets wasn't a good idea. The stark intensity of what I had experienced—what Barbara and I had felt—would take weeks of persistent work to erase. The echoes from murder weapons Worthington had given me in the past were nothing compared to experiencing a death firsthand.

And I had done that twice in a twelve-hour period.

But the scream haunted me. It lingered and echoed through my brain until I wanted to add my own voice to the pain and betrayal it carried so effectively.

Damning myself as a fool, I agreed to look into the murder.

CHAPTER FIVE

Tendrils of wet gray fog drifted across the forest road and took on the shape of crouching animals. I slowed, taking the sharp turns more carefully and avoiding the fog-beasts' mouths. In a stand of redwoods this thick, the slightest amount of fog made the slippery road a deathtrap. The BMW handled well as I smoothly slid around the curves and found a final straight stretch of road leading to the house.

I changed my mind about calling it a house as I pulled to a stop in front. It was nothing less than a low-slung mansion set in the trees. I closed my eyes and leaned back, listening hard. The sound of the nearby Pacific Ocean soothed me. I envied whoever owned the house. Living in such tranquility amid the forest and near the surf could do much to ease a troubled spirit.

Then I remembered why I had come and decided envy was not the exact emotion creeping through me. The owner of the mansion had died, Willie Worthington had said. Murdered. All the money-bought serenity in the world couldn't return a life to this world.

I got out of the car and walked slowly up the flagstone path. A knee-high rock wall lined the path on either side. Neatly tended grass sloped away into the foggy forest. From the front I couldn't see the ocean but did get doused by its continual spray. By the time I reached the elaborately carved wood double doors, I was drenched.

The uniformed California Highway Patrol officer stared at me as if I had turned to smoke. Only when I nodded and started past him did he respond.

"You another friend of the deceased?" he asked.

"I'm looking for the officer in charge. Detective Worthington suggested that I come out."

"I don't know a Worthington," the patrolman said suspiciously.

"SFPD."

The disgust on his face showed the rivalry between units. Away from the city, the San Francisco police were considered little more than members of a pussy posse, intent on busting vice rings and letting the real crimes go unsolved. Ask any CHP cop and he'd tell you about the real crimes being solved.

Ask any SFPD detective about the California Highway Patrol and you'd hear stories about radar traps and pulling over little old ladies with souped-up 'vettes.

"I'll get Cunningham." He turned to find his superior. I followed at a discreet distance, taking in the house and its decor as I went. Whoever had lived here had furnished with a lavish budget, if not taste matching mine.

The house itself was lovely and one designed to put a person at ease. Soft pastel walls, a thick earth-tone rug that made delicate love to every foot placed on it, the light airiness of the layout, all were superbly done. The knick-knacks cluttering shelves and tables everywhere ranged from primitive African art to neon sculptures and even a few Japanese pieces from the Heian Period. I couldn't help staring at the Danish modern furniture dating back to the 1950s, though. It was almost antique now. I couldn't imagine it had come back into vogue.

"Who the hell are you?" demanded a burly man, easily topping my six feet. He was broad-shouldered, trim-waisted and heavy, not an ounce of it fat. From the five-hundred-dollar suit he wore, it was hard to believe he was a California Highway Patrol officer.

"Peter Thorne." I thrust out my hand. He shook it reluctantly, his huge paw engulfing mine. "Detective Worthington suggested there might be points on the case that I could clarify for you. To be truthful, I'm not sure what those might be." I looked around. Rooms stretched off into the distance down a long hall, the same decor—or lack of it—apparent everywhere. The feel I got from the house was changing from the first impression of comfort. The dissonances multiplied and hinted at a resident who picked up pieces willy-nilly.

"Leonard Cunningham," the man said, staring at his hand as if he might have lost a finger or two in the exchange. After he had counted the digits twice and come up with the right number, he looked up. His watery blue eyes squinted as if he stared into a bright light. "You don't look like a freak."

"Thanks," I said dryly. I wondered what Worthington had told him. It didn't sound as if it was too complimentary.

"You touch things and come up with the murderer?"

The patrolman behind me snickered. Cunningham glared at him and sent him back to his post at the door to keep gawkers away, as if there would be any in this remote a location. It had taken me over an hour to drive across the Golden Gate Bridge and even find the appropriate back road leading here. The house's owner had wanted privacy and had been able to pay well for it.

"It's seldom that easy," I said. "Detective Worthington might have exaggerated my abilities. He did say you might need an expert on New Age artifacts. I might be more useful to you in that capacity."

"Yeah, right. This is a screwed-up mess." Cunningham turned and stalked into the living room. "Look at that. What do you make of it?" He pointed to ten burned stubs of red candles placed on a expensive mahogany table. I studied the pattern. The candles had been placed at the vertices of a five-pointed star.

"It's nothing to do with New Age mysticism," I said. "It might have been a pentagram used in a black mass."

"Witchcraft? Cults? The deceased was into things like that. You think it was witchcraft? We're getting a dozen reports a week from the fundamentalist crackpots about satanists taking over the schools, giving out undeserved parking tickets, crawling under their beds at night, the whole nine yards. Could this be devil worshippers?"

"I can't say. There's too little to go on." I reached out to touch a candle but caught myself before I touched the nearest waxy puddle. If the victim had performed a rite on this table, it was as likely to have been a satanic rite as one belonging to the peaceful and nature-cherishing wicca. I wanted to avoid further psychic shock unless it proved absolutely necessary.

"We don't think this had anything to do with the dame's death. This is history. Forensics says it's been here for several days."

I looked at the place again and nodded slowly. I had entered thinking it had been a woman who had died. Worthington hadn't said. And until now, Cunningham had not, either. In spite of the shotgun approach, the decor had a feel about it that didn't reflect a man's style.

With this added fact, I started looking around for things a woman might put on display. I didn't see any pictures of her or her loved ones.

"Did she have her photographs in another room?" I asked. "Perhaps the bedroom?"

"Photos? Don't remember seeing any," Cunningham said. He pulled out a notebook that might have been cloned from Worthington's and leafed through it. He shrugged. "No mention of photos in the inventory."

I looked around, hoping to find a dusty footprint showing where a picture frame had rested on a table. In this regard, the place was in perfect order. Whoever kept house did a good job. I idly considered asking for the name of the maid. My own place is cluttered beyond my ability to keep it up.

"You want to see where she got it?"

"Who was the woman? Worthington didn't tell me."

Cunningham's eyebrows arched up and then wiggled independently of one another. Such muscular control impressed me, even if it wasn't worth much this side of a circus sideshow.

"Thought you knew. Her name was Priscilla Santorini."

It was my turn to let my eyebrows wander upward, but they weren't able to perform the gyrations that Cunningham's had.

"She travelled in lofty circles," I said. Priscilla Santorini had been a well-known philanthropist among the high-society set. Other than seeing her name mentioned in the newspapers, I knew nothing about her. From the nature of the crime, it seemed almost impossible that I wasn't going to learn more than I really cared to.

"Yeah, she gave away tons of money to just about anyone asking for it. She shoveled the money into the pockets of the derelicts over in Frisco," Cunningham said with distinct distaste.

"Is there anything wrong with that?" I wondered if Cunningham had a suspect from the lower rungs of society's ladder. Priscilla Santorini might have offered aid to someone down on his luck and been murdered for it.

"As long as they stay in San Francisco, that's fine by me. I see people giving them money and the first thing they do is go buy cheap wine and get soused. You know where HQ is?"

I nodded. "It's just up Bryant Street from the Hall of Justice."

Cunningham made a face. "Yeah, on Eighth and Bryant, a couple blocks south of Market. You can't believe the beggars that hang around looking for a handout." Cunningham hitched up his trousers and lumbered around the room. The image of a bull in a china shop came to me. Somehow, Cunningham succeeded in missing the Chinese ceramic knickknacks on the tables by scant inches.

"She *was* murdered here?" I asked.

"Back in the bedroom. There's more of this kind of shit in a couple other rooms."

Cunningham pointed to the burnt candle stubs. As we went down the long hallway, I glanced into other bedrooms. From the appearance of the two rooms I saw, Priscilla Santorini kept them for guests. I followed Cunningham into the master bedroom.

"She lived alone," I said.

"Not on any given night, from what's being said about her. But you're right. She didn't have a permanent live-in."

On the dresser and on another table near her bed I found other implements hinting at cultist activity. I took a deep breath and let it out slowly. I was the wrong one to ask about witchcraft and what passed for its practice. I knew the historical traditions of wicca and something of the ancient rites, but only because they had interested me at one time. Modern belief in witchcraft varied according to the coven. Too many were simply bored men and women looking for an illicit religious thrill. Dancing around naked in the forest somehow enlivened their existence. Seeing some of them made me wonder why.

"The psychology of those dabbling in witchcraft is interesting," I said, testing what Cunningham wanted from me. "They mostly want personal recognition and are often rebelling against strict religious upbringing."

"Yeah, Catholics are the most prone toward getting into that kind of shit," Cunningham said. From his curt tone, he wanted nothing from me on the subject.

I wandered around the large bedroom, touching nothing. There was a disturbing coldness to the room. It raised gooseflesh on my upper arms, even though the temperature was warmer than I preferred.

Everywhere lay odd artifacts from a dozen different ancient religions. One table held a small library: The Egyptian Book of the Dead; a biography of Aleister Crowley; a short treatise on Zen by Master Suzuki; three pamphlets on crystal healing.

Cunningham saw my interest in the latter. "Those are the books I want some input about," he said.

I picked up one on the healing powers of red crystals and leafed through it. The curious coldness I experienced in the room permeated this book, also. I put it back and rubbed my hands together to warm them.

"Here's a picture of the deceased," Cunningham said, flipping through a folder he'd picked up from a nightstand. He passed over an eight-by-ten glossy of a lovely woman in her early thirties. Black hair fell softly to her shoulders, framing her white oval face, but it was her striking eyes that held my attention. They were colorless and seemed to be a window on eternity.

"She was one mean bitch, from the sound of it," Cunningham said. "Quite a looker, though."

"I really don't know how I can help you. I knew her only by reputation—and that's the reputation I read about in the papers."

"A real ball buster," he went on. "And the friends of

hers I've checked out all say she was heavily into the New Age shit.''

I handed the photo back. Cunningham tucked it into the file and passed over another photo. It took me by surprise. It was another shot of Priscilla Santorini, but this one had been taken by the medical examiner. I was glad it had been taken in black and white. A color photo would have made me lose my lunch.

"Brutal. Stabbed more than fifty times. The ME couldn't tell for sure which wound really killed her. Doesn't matter, really. Any of ten might have done it.''

"A psychopath did this,'' I murmured. The sight of the dead woman bothered me. The rage driving anyone to kill like this was both terrifying and intriguing. I had no idea what could spark such deadly passion.

"No shit, Sherlock.''

"I'm sorry. I'm wasting your time and my own. Worthington thought I might be able to help. I don't think so.''

"She was killed around ten-thirty this morning,'' Cunningham went on, as if he hadn't heard me. "This is the murder weapon. We found it beside the body.''

He reached down and lifted a plastic bag with a small tag on it. I saw the quartz-bladed knife and couldn't take my eyes off it. Depending on the artifact, I can get either a small hint of its owner or nothing. Usually, a deep trance is required to pick up the resonances of psychometry. There was a disturbing aura coming from the knife that drew me perversely, even as I tried to keep myself aloof.

I held out my hands and Cunningham dropped the blade flat across my palms.

The knife screamed and screamed and screamed.

CHAPTER SIX

The sound grew in intensity until I thought I was going deaf. I hadn't entered a meditation state and I still *heard* the knife's plaintive cries. Worse, they tore at my brain and threatened to rip me apart psychically. I tried to fight the evil influence, the sounds of agonizing death.

The knife clattered to the floor.

"Shit, if you're squeamish about holding a murder weapon, you should have told me." Leonard Cunningham bent and picked up the knife. I tried to apologize, but no words came to my lips.

"You look like hell. You want a drink of water? I'll get it, if you promise not to puke all over the place. The forensics team is supposed to come back tomorrow and give the place a second look."

"I'm all right," I said, even though I wasn't. I lifted my hands and stared as if blood dripped off them. The only lingering effect was one of intense psychic release. Physical effects were absent. My hands weren't burned and there wasn't any ringing in my ears. I simply stared at the knife Cunningham had retrieved after I had dropped it.

"You recognize it?" he asked, holding up the knife.

"You're right about it being a New Age artifact," I said. "Stores over in the city sell them for rituals. There's supposed to be great power locked in crystals. Quartz directs healing energy to the body, or it directs away negative energies such as anger and fear."

Cunningham cleared his throat. I thought he was going to spit. Instead, he said, "This didn't work for her. It ripped through her enough times to make the bed a bloody mess."

I looked at the bed. The bedclothes had been stripped away. The mattress pad was a pale pink and hid the huge blot of blood well. To my surprise, I felt none of the vertigo that had hit me earlier. Only the knife carried the psychic charge.

"It's the murder weapon," I said. "There's no doubt about it."

"Of course not," Cunningham said. "Forensics decided on that right away. The glassy edge matches the tears on the wounds good enough for immediate verification."

I started to tell him what I heard. Something told me to hold back, if only for a while.

"You look like hell. Are you sure you're all right? I got work to do."

"I'm fine. What do you need to know about the knife?" I found myself staring at it as if it pulled me into a trance.

"We found some other shit around here I don't understand—more than the candle wax out on the table. There were brass pendulums in a couple places."

"Simple pendulums, not crystal ones?"

He shrugged. That meant they weren't anything elaborate like this knife. I stared at it again and blinked. The power locked in it!

"Radionics is a diagnostic technique using a pendulum. The healer asks the pendulum questions and it swings back and forth."

"Can it tell me who'll win the World Series? I got a bet on the Giants every year, and I always lose."

"It's not supposed to predict the future. Radionics is more for inner power than outer."

"Too bad. I've lost a couple hundred over the years on those bums." Cunningham held up a pendulum and let it swing. "How's it work?"

"You ask the question. The answer comes either in back-and-forth swings or in a circular swing. One way means yes and the other no."

"Sort of a dangling Ouija board?"

"Something like that," I said. "But it's for healing."

"Didn't do Santorini any good. Where can you get junk like this?"

I stared at the crystal knife. A part of New Age mysticism deals with aura balancing, a technique meant to stimulate and balance the electromagnetic field surrounding a living body. Somehow, the knife had absorbed much of Priscilla Santorini's life force. In its milky depths a porof the woman still lived. The screaming might be her spirit trying to escape.

Or was it the murderer's psychic energy imprinted on the blade?

I shook that off. Some of the New Age teachings make sense to me. The explanations and reasons aren't always right for me, but there is more to it than the skeptics claim. The meditative trance that allows me to psychometrize is a type of rebirthing. My breathing is controlled and the trance lets me walk an astral plane closed to most people. I've never returned to face my birth trauma—I'm not sure I'd want to—but it feels possible once on that other plane.

"You got a thing for this knife? You see others like it?" demanded Cunningham.

"It . . . draws me," I said lamely.

"Worthington said you touch things and tell details about it. Is that what happened? You touched the knife and you saw something?"

"It's hard to explain. I usually enter a self-induced trance to 'see' details. The knife is so strongly charged with psychic energy, spirit, soul, if you will, that I don't have to enter the meditative state to hear it."

"Hear it?"

I swallowed hard. Cunningham wasn't going to believe me. I told him anyway. "It screams. I've never heard anything more soul-shattering in my life."

"Bullshit." He cleared his throat and looked as if he wanted to spit again. Then he thrust the knife toward me. "Take it. Tell me what you see in it. Tell me something the forensics boys can't."

In everyone reside self-destructive impulses. For some, they overwhelm the need to live. The person commits suicide, or lives a life trying to find suitably violent ways of dying. Skydiving, rock climbing, race car driving, other sports fit this mold. At other times normally sane people do insanely destructive things.

I took the knife.

My hands trembled. Waves of pain and sheer terror washed through me. I fought to control it, to rise above it. I should have entered my trance before accepting the knife. I fought to find the tranquil state, the equanimity of soul needed to cope with the message of death and torment locked within the vibrating atoms of the quartz knife.

For what stretched to an eternity, I fought to control my rebellious, frightened spirit. Getting over my inner fear of death allowed me to slip onto the astral plane where I had been so recently with Barbara Chan.

The screams echoed across this distant, yet near landscape. The shrieks turned to eye-searing red and orange. I smelled the sound, then tasted it. I spat. It burned as if my tongue had been cut and salt sprinkled on it.

Beyond all this, the depths of the knife opened, a television being turned on. A picture formed and I found myself drawn into it, falling, crying out and having my voice lost in the agonized cries from the crystal knife.

I loved you. How can you do this to me?

Pain. Twisting, horrible pain as the knife slides in. Heart ruptures. Spleen is cut in half. The lungs. Drowning. Blood flooding the lungs.

You slut. You whore. I loved you!

I doubled over, unable to accept any more of the punishment. I was dying. My inner organs were slashed to bloody fragments. And still the cutting crystal knife sought my flesh.

A hard fist knocked me flat onto the floor. I lay on my back, staring at the ceiling. Tiny stars twinkled. For a second I thought I had been transported from the room and saw the nighttime sky. Then the tiny spots came into sharper focus. The twinkling was of lights implanted in Priscilla Santorini's bedroom ceiling. She could lie in her bed and watch the constellations wheel through the ersatz sky.

She could lie under her lover and watch the stars over his shoulder.

"I told you not to puke. You aren't going to, are you? You'd better get the hell on out of here." Leonard Cunningham sounded worried. He didn't want to fill out another report. A society doyenne's death gave him headaches enough. It wouldn't be long before the newspapers clamored for a quick solution to the brutal crime.

"Male. Priscilla Santorini's killer was male. I heard him. Husky voice usually, but it turned shrill when he attacked her with the knife." I stared at the murder

weapon. Again I had dropped it rather than continue to
endure its psychic punishment.

"Yeah? Tell me more."

"A jilted lover. It had to be. He called her a slut and
claimed she was unfaithful."

"Santorini's love life was like a Who's Who in San
Francisco. Who she *didn't* fuck is a shorter list than who
she did."

"He loved her," I said, barely hearing Cunningham.
"There might have been a lover's triangle. I'm trying to
remember what I experienced. It all comes in so fast. It's
hard to sort it out." My temples began to throb with a
Mt. Vesuvius of a headache.

"You don't know?"

"Impressions," I said. "I get a torrent of impressions.
Sometimes I interpret them according to the way I think
they ought to be rather than what is really there." I composed myself. Sweat poured down my face. My suit was
drenched and my hands still shook. Never had I encountered an artifact this powerfully charged with psychic energy. It overwhelmed me and I found myself beginning to
hate it, both for what it did to me and what it failed to do.

I wanted to conquer it, yet knew I couldn't. It was too
dominant. Standing against a tsunami would be easier.

"So it might not be a guy who felt pissed that she
bounced him for another guy?"

"He loved her. That's not in question," I said. "I can't
say if that's why he killed her. There might be more. There
must be more."

"Why's that?" Cunningham sounded amused.

"I've touched wedding rings of newlyweds and those
married for fifty years. The passion is different. This man,
the killer, with him it's not the same."

"Most killers are different. Otherwise, we'd all be out
murdering each other all the time." Cunningham snorted.
"Hell of it is, I'm not sure if that's not the way it's becoming. This is one fucking messy case."

"He—the killer—knew his way around this place. But
there are others. I keep getting the feeling she was engaged in a *ménage à trois.*"

"That might have been good enough for the killer,"

said Cunningham. "He might not have known and then got mad about it."

"No," I said slowly. Images formed and vanished even as I thought about all I had experienced while holding the knife. "He approved. He was a part of her life, yet he wasn't. I don't understand this."

"She was one sick puppy, that's what I understand. You get anything about drugs?" Cunningham asked suddenly.

"Only the cocaine she kept in the head of her bed," I said. My eyes widened as the words slipped out. I hadn't known that I knew that.

"Where?" Cunningham was all cop again.

I looked at the headboard. I shook my head. It was there somewhere, but I didn't know where. The killer had stopped Priscilla Santorini from opening the secret panel. She had wanted to snort a line with him, but the woman's slayer had used the opening to snatch up the knife from the bedside table and drive it between her shoulder blades.

"There," I said, pointing toward the right side of the headboard. "It's there somewhere."

"Son of a bitch," Cunningham said. He tapped the side of the wood frame and a tiny door popped open. Inside he found a bag containing several grams of white powder. "How did you find this when the forensics boys missed it?"

"She was reaching for it when she was stabbed. The first thrust took her in mid-back. It didn't kill her. She screamed and turned over. The rest of the stabs caught her in the chest and neck and belly."

"You got all that by going into a trance and holding the knife?"

"I have an alibi for the time of the death."

"Yeah, I just bet you do." Cunningham stared at the tiny cache of coke. "What do you think of a drug deal gone sour?"

"It . . . doesn't seem right," I said lamely.

"So what does, Thorne? What feels right to you about this?"

I stared at the crystal knife on the floor, then looked up at Leonard Cunningham. "Nothing feels right about it," I answered.

CHAPTER SEVEN

Earl Grey tea soothed my nerves. I hardly realized how upset simply touching the crystal knife had made me. The tea should have pumped needed stimulants into my blood. Paradoxically, the theophylline and caffeine let me sit without shaking. The past two days had been a never-ending nightmare for me. And because I had told Lieutenant Cunningham I would look into possible sources for the quartz murder weapon, the next few days wouldn't give me a chance to rest, either.

Having psychometric powers wears me down both physically and emotionally more than anyone lacking the talent—or curse—can imagine. Knowing someone's deepest, darkest secret puts me in the same class as a Peeping Tom, except I do it through the windows of the soul.

The man who killed Priscilla Santorini had a sick, sick soul, and looking at it made me feel dirty.

I finished the cup of tea and poured another. The warmth rested in my belly and turned me almost mellow. I doodled on a yellow pad of legal-sized paper, not caring what came out of my personal Rorschach test. Between the work for Worthington and Cunningham, I had exhausted myself. And the black cloud that threatened to crush me still hovered nearby after Barbara Chan's experiment.

Of the three, that was least threatening and, in its way, the most intriguing. A man killing his wife lacked subtly or challenge. The crystal knife frightened me more than I wanted to admit. But the shovel I had held tried to reveal mysteries to me that I was unable to see—and which seemed to slip just beyond my grasp. It was this nearness that kept me coming back to the images billowing from the shovel.

The doorbell rang. I sighed. Whoever called wasn't likely to find me a congenial companion. When I find myself drained mentally, I need to get away from people and recharge my mental batteries.

I peered through the small peephole and saw Barbara Chan in the hall. I opened the door. She looked at me, a curiously beguiling combination of little girl and mature woman.

"Peter?"

"Come in," I said. It surprised me. I had thought I wanted to be alone. Seeing her changed that.

"I don't want to interrupt. You keep odd hours."

"I didn't sleep much last night," I said. "Would you like a cup of tea?"

"Sure. That's okay. I'll get it. You want some more?" She stood on tiptoe and peered down at my cup on the end table. It was almost empty.

"Fill 'er up," I said. "What brings you back?"

"I didn't know if you'd want to see me." Before I could answer, she rushed on. "That was scary, what you did with me the other day. It's made me think a lot. I want to know everything I can about the trance state that lets you walk across the astral plane."

I closed my eyes and heard—smelled, saw, tasted, felt—the death scream.

"Peter? Are you sure you're all right? You turned pale when I mentioned that."

"I found out what caused . . . the sound we experienced." I hesitated at calling it a sound since the senses are jumbled when in a trance. The aura from each object I touch is different. The power trapped in the crystal knife told eloquently of the stark emotion between killer and victim.

Barbara stared at me, her eyes dark and large and again curiously childlike. She hung on my every word. I wondered if this was what the best teachers felt. There was a combination of adoration and even awe in her gaze, yet it was I who should be in awe of her. She worked on an advanced degree in physics, had both a physical and a spiritual beauty lacking in so many these days and possessed a personality I found totally captivating.

In a way, this was a part of what I felt when I performed. Every eye was on me, but each performance was different. They were games, challenges between stage magician and audience. They tried to catch me and see how the tricks were done. I wiggled my fingers and looked in the wrong direction while my clever hands produced miracles that were nothing but deceptions. But always it was an adversarial process, me against their sharp eyes.

"What was it?" she asked.

I told her about Priscilla Santorini, fearing that she would be repulsed. If anything, Barbara was intrigued. She glowed with vitality and accepted this as a challenge rather than an ugly experience to be hidden away.

"So she died while we listened. Fascinating," she said, raising one eyebrow just like Spock. "I'm not trained in this. Whatever I got came through you and your powers. Do you think I would be able to feel anything if I touched the crystal knife?"

"It's the most powerful artifact I've ever encountered," I said. "You might get some of the impressions, but I don't recommend trying. The crime was . . . bloody." It sounded lame, and it was. I made no apologies for wanting to keep the details from her. The stark emotion and raw intensity of the hatred mingled with the thwarted love was not something to face unless it was necessary.

Not for the first time, I asked myself why *I* found it necessary to continue. Cunningham was able to ask the same questions I would. He might take longer, but he would get to the dealers in the New Age articles eventually. The city was not his domain, but others would be more than willing to help. Priscilla Santorini had been well known and respected in San Francisco society circles.

I kept wondering about Cunningham's allegations about her sexual proclivities. How many of those society contacts had been her lovers? One might even be the murderer.

"So what do we do?" asked Barbara. She put her hands on her knees and bent forward, intent on the chase.

"You want to come with me?" The idea of having her accompany me was pleasant. I had expected to wander around poking here and there by myself until something surfaced.

"I was going to see if anyone remembered selling the quartz knife to her. There might be hundreds of them sold, but she was a striking woman. A clerk might remember her—or even recognize her from pictures."

"If, as you say, she was into all sorts of odd cult things, she might have been a regular customer wherever she got the knife. That might give us a lead on her murderer," Barbara said. "Where do we start?"

"By finishing off our tea," I said, doing as I instructed. We decided it was easier to reach the Columbus and Grant area on the bus from my apartment on Bret Harte Terrace. I didn't want to walk the four blocks to where my car was garaged, then not find parking anywhere near the stores selling the crystals and other implements.

It seemed to startle Barbara that I suggested the bus.

"Silly," she muttered. "I guess I thought you could teleport yourself across town."

"I'm only a poor psychometrician," I pleaded, but this bothered me. It meant she thought of my powers as freakish—and maybe of me as a freak. Often I play on this perception in others. With Barbara Chan, I didn't want to.

We exchanged small talk until we reached the northern edge of Chinatown. We got off the bus and took a shortcut down Adler Street and out to the intersection of Columbus and Broadway. The City Lights Bookstore wasn't far off, but I ignored it this time. My interest lay in other stores.

"How about that one?" she asked, pointing to a store with a crudely lettered sign.

"Rolfing is hidden under the New Age umbrella," I said, "but near so many sex shops and sex shows, it's likely to be a massage parlor in the classic sense."

"I'm not even sure what rolfing is," she said, "but it does sound dirty."

At that I laughed. "It's nothing more than a deep massage of the joints. The idea behind it is that unresolved trauma lodges there until the massage releases them."

"Tense muscles are a part of life," she said. "My shoulders knot up all the time. When I'm working in the lab, it's all I can do sometimes to keep from crying."

"I'll show you some of the techniques later," I said.

"Is that a promise?" Barbara grinned widely.

I told her that it was, and meant it. We started down Columbus and looked into a half dozen different stores. Most of the clerks were the store owners and denied having sold anything to Priscilla Santorini. One or two looked shocked when I mentioned the name; they recognized her, but I got no sense that she was a regular customer.

"How many of the damned stores are there?" complained Barbara after an hour of walking. "You'd think one set of crystals would be as good as another."

"For all practical purposes, they are. I don't think they do any more than aid in meditation. How quartz can cure or a copper grid can bring your aura into alignment escapes me."

"I thought you believed all this."

"Some," I said. "Not much, though."

"You can psychometrize and you still don't believe it?" The idea startled her.

"I do believe we are in a time of changes and that we can move closer to perfection. That's the point where I part company with most New Age believers."

"There's another store," Barbara Chan said. "How many more do we check out?"

I knew of almost a dozen more scattered around the city. This area simply had the highest concentration of stores. Leonard Cunningham was getting a lot of free work out of me.

"We can knock off for lunch after we check it out. We can hop the Mason cable car and in ten minutes be at a great Italian place I know."

I stopped and then smiled broadly when I saw the man working on a small display outside the store.

"It's been a while since you were in business, hasn't it, Ross?" I asked.

The short, stout man looked up, startled. He grinned when he saw me and thrust out his hand. I shook it, squeezing down hard, knowing he'd try to break my hand with his grip.

"I've followed your career, Peter. You've done well for yourself. You working now?"

"I've got a gig coming up in a couple weeks," I said.

"A small one, nothing important. Need to find a new assistant and get the bugs out of a new act."

"A small gig? A thousand a week? Two?" he asked.

"Closer to the latter," I admitted. "When did you hang up the magic wand and start the store? This is your place, isn't it?" I stared at the sign proudly proclaiming this to be the pyramid headquarters for all San Francisco.

"I couldn't stand the travelling," he said. "The wife's been ailing and didn't want to come with me anymore. You know how hard it is getting a new assistant. I figured, what the hell. I'm no spring chicken. I'd run a magic supply store way back in the old days. Why not do it again, you know?"

"I remember getting some of my first equipment from you down in L.A.," I said. "What are you doing selling New Age . . ."

"Shit?" Ross said, smiling crookedly. "There's money in it right now. I met up with some guys over in Colorado that supply me quartz and other crystals. There's nothing like it in the entire town. I have 'em flocking in to buy it." Ross shook his head. "Bunch of weirdos, but they got money."

The man looked from me to Barbara and said hastily, "Not that a true believer is a weirdo."

"That's all right. I don't know that much about it," Barbara said.

"She's just along for the ride, Ross," I said. He looked relieved that he hadn't offended a possible customer.

"You're not into the New Age crap, are you, Peter? You were always pretty level-headed."

"I'm trying to track down the source of a quartz knife."

"I've got the best selection in town. Some of the New Age surgeons, and I use the term loosely, use them for their operations. They're supposed to let the patient heal fifty percent faster. Bullshit, all of it, but they believe, so I sell. No harm in that."

"Was Priscilla Santorini one of your customers?"

"A slick-looking lady in her mid-thirties? Long, black hair and the most vivid blue eyes you've ever seen? So blue they looked transparent? Sure, she comes in all the time. If half my customers spent what she does, I could retire.''

"What sort of items did she buy?''

"She bought everything, and I mean everything. I gave up trying to follow her tastes. You know, with some of them, you can tell what they're into. Not with her. She would come in and buy entire cases of crystals.''

"What about crystal knives?''

"You mentioned that before,'' Ross said, turning wary for the first time. "She didn't hurt herself any with one of my knives, did she?''

We wandered into the store and I looked over my old friend's stock. In a display case near the door were a half dozen knives similar to the one used to kill Priscilla Santorini.

"She didn't hurt herself with it,'' I said. Ross let out a sigh of relief. "Did you think she would?''

"Naw, not really, but she was into kinky stuff, I think. Her shopping bag fell open when she was in here a few months ago. It had all kinds of bondage equipment in it. A pair of handcuffs, some leather harnesses, you know.''

I said nothing. The silence caused Ross to grow uneasy again.

"You sure she didn't hurt herself? Quartz carries quite an edge.''

"She didn't spill a drop of her own blood,'' I said. "Someone did it for her.''

CHAPTER EIGHT

I found it hard to concentrate as I sat across the table from Barbara. We had left Ross's store and caught a cable car to the Italian restaurant on Mason. It had closed a week earlier, so we settled on a small bistro nestled in a corner under Coit Tower looking east past the Bay Bridge.

What distracted me even more was Barbara Chan.

"What do we do now? We've found where she got the knife."

"That's a start, but it doesn't help too much," I said, forcing my thoughts away from the woman and to the problem. "Santorini bought her own murder weapon."

"It's too bad your friend never saw her come in with anyone. That might tie someone in to the murder."

"That's Cunningham's problem, not mine. Not *ours*. Thanks for coming along like this. You didn't have to."

"I wanted to, Peter. It's been, well, not fun exactly, but I enjoyed poking through the stores."

"Have you learned anything?"

"About New Age philosophy, sure, a little. But it doesn't have much to do with your talent, does it?"

"I don't think so. The meditation techniques are alike, but then I learned them from other stage magicians and a Zen master. The similarities are inherent in putting yourself into a trance."

"Does it really exhaust you when you touch objects?" Her dark eyes locked with mine. I took her hands.

"I usually have to go into the meditative state before I can psychometrize in depth. The knife is the first object I've ever found that has been so overpoweringly strong."

She squeezed my hands. "It might be a good thing you can't get any picture right now," she said.

"I'm getting a fine one." I bent closer. "Lunch is served."

She jerked back guiltily, a small child caught rummaging through her mother's closet. Barbara looked up at the waiter and flashed him a bright smile. He was as charmed by her as I was.

We ate in silence for a few minutes, my thoughts wandering. She brought me back when she asked, "Are you going to psychometrize the knife again?"

"It wouldn't do any good. The images are too strong, and they upset me in ways I can't put into words."

"Like the shovel in my experiment?"

"Worse," I said. "I touched the knife and heard the cries, and deep inside a part of me died along with Priscilla Santorini. I can't explain it. There is an incredible psychic energy locked in the blade. It's dangerous just being near it—dangerous for my sanity."

"Is it because it's quartz and there is something to the New Age belief in its power?"

"Possibly. I try not to examine these matters too closely. It's as if I'm a tight-wire walker. If I'm thinking of other things, I can walk just fine. The instant I start to wonder how it is possible to remain balanced on a tiny wire, I start wobbling."

"Do you think I can design an experiment that will reveal the source of your power?"

"I had hoped for some insight when I agreed to be a guinea pig. I'm sorry I did now, except for one thing."

"Oh, and what's that?"

I just grinned at her. She smiled back and I knew that her experiment hadn't been a complete waste, even if it had needlessly burdened me with a psychic cloud.

"Let's finish lunch and get some idea what Priscilla Santorini was up to," I said.

"Isn't it obvious? Your friend said she bought crystals and bondage gear."

"That's not an obvious combination to me," I said. "She didn't seem interested in anything but the New Age implements in Ross's store. He said she pointedly ignored the witchcraft paraphernalia."

"So?"

I explained about the burnt candles on Priscilla Santorini's table. "She did a rite there, and it had nothing to do with healing or crystal lore or meditation."

"Do you think the killer might have sacrificed her?"

Barbara had hit on a question that had been working its way to the surface of my mind but hadn't taken full form. I nodded. Events fit together better this way. The woman was savagely killed by a lover, who performed a blood rite afterward.

"No," I said suddenly. "That's not what went on there. The killer showed too much passion during the murder."

"Maybe he relented and tried to save her soul."

Who knew what strange thoughts went through the mind of a murderer, especially one steeped in cultist beliefs. I wished I could take the crystal knife and truly see what had happened. The notion turned me cold inside. In some ways, I'd *become* the killer when I shared the moment of blood. That frightened me. How could I ever know I'd be able to shake off the fire that burned within the slayer and return to my own more pacific existence?

"We need to know more about her friends before any progress can be made," I said. "Who shared her New Age philosophy—and who didn't."

"Could her death have been the result of a falling out over philosophy?"

"I doubt it. While that might be a part—say the murderer wanted to drift more toward satanism than Priscilla Santorini—the root of the motive lies in love."

"In hate, you mean," corrected Barbara.

I wasn't sure what I meant. The emotions locked within the quartz blade were too strong for easy interpretation.

"Let's finish lunch," I said.

"And then?"

Her foot crept up my leg under the table. Then I felt even more, and it had nothing to do with her placing an electrode there.

My apartment on Russian Hill has a fine view of the city, day or night. Barbara agreed, on both counts.

CHAPTER NINE

"Who's she?" asked Lieutenant Cunningham, looking past me to where Barbara Chan stood.

"She's a research assistant at the University of San Francisco," I said. When this didn't satisfy him, I added, "She's a friend of mine."

Cunningham cleared his throat and leaned back in his swivel chair. The California Highway Patrol office, less than a mile from the blue-roofed Marin County Courthouse designed by Frank Lloyd Wright, had been fussed over by an expert interior decorator. Every color blended harmoniously and not a slip of paper was out of place. I wondered how a busy man like Cunningham managed to keep the clutter down. He must have been reading my mind—or at least my expression.

"I've got a cleaning woman who comes in daily. She and my secretary go through the stuff on the desk to make sure it's nothing important. It's either tossed or filed. Being stationed in Marin County has its compensations." He cleared his throat, then added, "That's the way business is done out here. If you don't walk the walk, you're scum and nobody talks to you."

That explained the expensive suits the lieutenant wore. I wondered how he afforded such clothing on a California Highway Patrol salary—or if such things were shifted to an expense account.

"I suppose everyone expects you to look as prosperous as they are," said Barbara.

"More," Cunningham assured her. He leaned forward, thick arms on the clean surface of the heavily polished desk. "What did you get on the knife? Anything worth mentioning?"

"It was bought at a store just off Columbus and Broadway," I said. "A friend of mine named Ross runs the store and remembered Santorini. She was a good customer—but only for the New Age paraphernalia. She didn't bother with candles and the other witchcraft implements.''

"Not at his store, at least," sighed Cunningham. "The more I dig into this, the weirder it gets. You just never know about people. She led one hell of a fragmented life."

"What do you mean?" I had hints of her sexual preferences and thought I knew what the lieutenant was getting at.

"Her charity work was separate from the high-society whirl. They seemed to overlap only because that's the kind of shit the columnists eat up. Santorini kept them distinctly separate."

"The rest of her life was compartmentalized like that, too," I guessed. "Her business dealings were separate from everything else, as were her New Age dealings."

"I'm finding some casual connections. It's impossible not to," said Cunningham. "Her business manager might have been mixed up with her in a sexual way, but it's hard to pin down right now. He's denying it as if his life depended on it."

"Does it?" I asked. Barbara moved closer and stood beside me. I appreciated her presence. Cunningham's office made me uneasy. For all its tasteful decoration, it lacked any hint of the man's personality. It was cold and foreboding here. Getting out of the office seemed more important than anything else at the moment.

"Yeah, it might. His alibi for the morning of the murder is pretty shaky. But he's not the only fish on the line. The problem is the same as with most of the felony crimes out here."

"The suspects usually live out of your jurisdiction," I guessed.

"SFPD cooperates. Hell, Worthington sent you to bedevil me, didn't he?"

"I've done what I can," I said. "Ross is a friend, and he'll be glad to answer any other questions you might have."

"He doesn't sell any of the B and D stuff, does he?"

"He saw her once or twice with new, uh, bindings."

"Handcuffs, chains, restraints." Cunningham let out

another deep sigh. "This killing might have a bondage motive. She had boxes full of kinky leather stuff in every closet in the house."

"There's that much different . . ." began Barbara. Her voice trailed off when both of us looked at her. "Sorry," she said contritely. "I went to school over in Berkeley and thought I'd heard or seen just about everything."

"Lady, you haven't seen one percent of it," Cunningham said. "You ought to hang around here for a day or two—or go sit in the SFPD squad room. The Hall of Justice is teeming with flakes and fucking kinks. It doesn't take long for you to realize you ain't learned nothing about the world."

I started to leave. The unemotional room was sucking away at my spirit. If I tried to psychometrize the knick-knacks in the room, I'd end up visualizing myself trapped in the Arctic.

Barbara stopped me. "There's nothing more we can do?" she asked Cunningham.

"What do you want to do, lady?"

"The knife is psychically charged," she said. I didn't want her rattling on too much. Cunningham believed I could sense the killer through the knife. My involvement with Priscilla Santorini's death was at an end.

"So?"

"So is it possible to examine it again?"

"Barbara! No!" I couldn't make my disapproval more emphatic. She ignored me. So did Cunningham.

"You got the talent he claims?" asked Cunningham. He eyed her like a specimen under a microscope. Barbara seemed oblivious to it. She was caught up in wanting to try her own ability on the knife.

"Not really, but if you're finished with the knife, my graduate advisor might be able to turn up something. He's Dr. David Michaelson. He's a physicist."

"I've heard the name somewhere," said Cunningham, scratching his chin. "Since I don't read much besides crime reports and the newspapers—damned near the same thing these days—I must have come across it there."

"The newspaper?" I asked, amused at Barbara's expression. Even hinting that Michaelson was a criminal upset her. She didn't appreciate Cunningham's sense of humor.

"Must have been, now that I think about it."

"He can run tests on the knife. He might be able to tell more than your forensics team."

"The chances of that are slim and none," Cunningham said. "They're damned good at their work."

"Did they find that the killer was a male?" asked Barbara.

"We don't know that. The ferocity of the attack makes it likely, but a strong woman could have used the knife. It's got one hell of a sharp blade."

"Let Dr. Michaelson try. He and Peter are engaged in a series of experiments on psychometrizing."

"One of the rocket scientist types actually believes it?" Cunningham snorted in disgust. "He's got cobwebs in his head from being in his ivory tower too long."

I tried to get a word in and failed. I didn't like Barbara giving the California Highway Patrol the idea that her advisor approved of me. A single conversation with Michaelson would put us all in a dark, dark shadow.

"If you're done mixing metaphors, can we examine the knife?" Barbara was almost breathless at the possibility. I wasn't sure if she really intended for Michaelson to work on the knife, or if she thought she could glean something from it if she entered a trance state.

"What do you say about this?" Cunningham looked right at me. His eyes bored through to my soul. I needed inanimate objects to delve into their owner's head. Cunningham did it directly.

"I'm only Dr. Michaelson's guinea pig." It sounded lame to me, especially since it was a lie.

"We might be able to release the knife. It's been gone over as good as anybody can do. The paper work will be a bitch since there's no reason for this Michaelson to even look at a piece of evidence from a capital crime."

"I'll herd it along," promised Barbara.

"We'll see."

"Thanks, Lieutenant."

"Wait a minute," Cunningham said as we turned to leave. "Aren't you going to ask who I'm investigating?"

"This ends my connection with the case. I did Worthington a favor in stopping by. I'm sorry I couldn't do more for you."

"How'd you do Worthington any favors?" Cunningham asked, curious.

"He wanted to know if there was any connection with drugs in this case."

"He's after Steve Hackett, too?"

I sighed. That had been the name Worthington had asked me to be on the alert for.

"Who else is involved?" I asked. I owed Worthington whatever I could find. But there it ended.

"Here's a list of the people under suspicion, Thorne." Cunningham held up a neatly typed roster. "I don't suppose you'd like to take a gander at it?"

I laughed without too much humor. "I don't need to see it any closer. I just memorized it." My act included several mentalist tricks which required me to recite long lists of facts prepared by assistants. No one believed I could read the lists in the short time usually given, much less remember them. Several years of intense training made it almost second nature to me now.

This startled Cunningham. He started to protest, then leaned back and looked at me with something approaching admiration.

"I'll just bet you did memorize it. So go do something about it. And we'll see about sending Michaelson the crystal knife for tests. And don't bother me with any of this, unless Worthington tells you to, all right? Since Santorini got offed, I've got a report on a burglary ring working on high-ticket thefts, not to mention a pair of guys fresh in from Vacaville boosting any car with a funny Italian name plastered on it in chrome."

He thought I was Willie Worthington's pawn. I didn't correct him. I'd report Steven Hackett's presence on the suspect list and that would end my obligation.

I wondered why I didn't believe that.

CHAPTER TEN

Organs died in a liquid rush. The pain! Too much. I tasted it, I smelled it, I heard the crystal knife driving into my guts. The razor-sharp edge slashed and cut and drove deeper.

I love you! I hate you! I hate!

The knife refused to leave my hands. I tried to drop it, get rid of it as I had done the shovel. It stuck to me like epoxy. Pain inside my head mounted until I tasted blood and salt and fear. I was dying—and I was still inside the mind of the killer.

Such hatred of Priscilla! Such self-hatred!

"Do something," came the distant words. I knew they were spoken in the real world, not the world of the astral plane where the aura from the crystal knife resided. Frost formed around me, sounding green and chili-pepper hot. I heard it all.

And the scream. Everywhere echoed the agonized shrieking of the crystal blade in my hands. No matter how I turned and twisted and dodged on the astral plane, it followed like a bloodhound.

Then it ended. Silence came so abruptly that it hurt my ears, both physical and psychic.

"Peter?" A hand shook me. I tried to respond. My muscles were locked in a rictus of pain and fear. Truly I had been inside the mind of the man murdering Priscilla Santorini. And the hatred of both the woman and himself was overwhelming. Crying in rage and frustration would accomplish nothing. But I did anyway.

"What's wrong with him?" The question wasn't sympathetic.

"The knife is a powerful psychic battery, Dr. Michaelson. Peter taps into it and it . . . drains him," Barbara finished lamely. "I don't have the words to describe it."

"Neither does he. Look at the readouts. We hooked everything to him in the lab. There was no change in his basal metabolism. He's faking again, Barbara. Hell, you said the equipment in the ER was faulty. It might have been. The damned doctors don't know how to maintain their own equipment. But this is *mine*. It works as good as any you'll find."

"Look at him, Doctor. How can you say he's pretending?"

"Look at the readouts. How can you tell me he's *not?*"

David Michaelson snorted in contempt. "You're supposed to keep an objective view, Barbara. Assume he is faking. What readings would you expect? This is getting us nowhere. Drop this or I'll have to recommend your finding another advisor."

Barbara Chan looked frustrated. She glanced from me to the physicist across the room. He bent over a black-topped work table laden with equipment. Most of the instruments bore little resemblance to anything I'd ever seen. They might have been fakes for all I knew. If the placebo effect has to be taken into account for medical experiments, why not use fake apparatus for paranormal ones?

"I'm all right," I told Barbara. My hands still trembled. Worst of all was the foul taste in my mouth. I wanted to spit, but there was nowhere decent for me to get rid of the bile.

I used a handkerchief and found a dollop of blood there. I had bitten my tongue.

Barbara held the knife in front of her, her expression slightly sick as if she got some measure of the evil locked within its crystal structure, too.

"Don't give it back. I can't handle it," I told her.

"You put on quite a show, Thorne," said Michaelson. "See this strip?" He held up a thin strip of paper that had run through a recorder. The pen had traced out a wavy line that didn't vary in amplitude more than two gradations.

"Is this my EEG tracing?"

"Galvanic skin response. It's part of a so-called lie detector rig. The resistance of your skin's surface will change as you sweat. Telling a lie produces a physiologic response. There is no change in your GSR."

"Why not hook me up to a lie detector and ask me what I experienced? That ought to show you I'm telling the truth."

Michaelson shook his head. "People can firmly believe black is white and pass a lie detector test. Delusions are real, if you believe in them hard enough."

I looked at Barbara. She still held the quartz blade as if it might explode. She placed it on the table and backed off. I wondered if she had felt some small tingling from the energy and hatred locked inside. She must have. She had heard it scream when it was being used to kill Priscilla Santorini.

"There's nothing remarkable about the knife, either," Michaelson went on. "I've tried every test I can think of—and a dozen suggested by colleagues."

"He did some X-ray work on it," Barbara told me. "Back-scattering, a full crystal structure, even transmission work using a high-intensity e-beam. There's nothing remarkable about the knife."

"I even did some NMR work on it, thinking there might be something to you sensing a resonance inherent in the structure. I was careful when I took the blade down to superconducting temperatures. It didn't do any good."

"Null results," Barbara said. "That doesn't mean anything, Doctor. Quartz isn't a good specimen for nuclear resonance work."

"It's a piezoelectric," said Michaelson.

"That might be why it retains a psychic image," Barbara argued, almost pleading. Strictly on debating points, she was losing. I had no idea what she or her advisor were talking about.

"The notion of a psychic transducer is ridiculous," scoffed Michaelson. "There's no evidence for it. Where are the electrodes needed for creating either a transverse or longitudinal wave? Nowhere, that's where. RF frequencies? There aren't any."

"Dr. Michaelson, we are supposed to be trying to find out these things."

I saw that her protest fell on an adamantine mind. David

Michaelson sneered slightly and said, "Do you want to believe in an ether? Does his mental talent translate along some unknown material to impinge on his mind?"

"What did you discover about the knife?" I broke in. "Was there anything unusual about it?"

"Not structurally. The edges were chipped," Michaelson said. I saw that I had him off his jeremiad. "That is understandable from the description of the crime. Even quartz will flake off when it hits human bone hard enough."

"I meant, did you find any electromagnetic residue? Anything that might give a hint about the source of the scream when I touch it?"

"There's nothing," he said with some pleasure.

"Doctor, I—" Barbara started to speak, then bit off the words. "I'm sorry. I don't think I can continue as your assistant on this project."

Michaelson's eyes widened. "Do you know what you're throwing away?"

"I might leave the university," she said, tears forming in the corners of her almond-shaped, dark eyes.

"That won't be necessary," I said hastily. "I don't want to cause dissension in the ranks."

"I don't want to lose you, Barbara," said Michaelson. "You've got talent, aptitude, you—"

"I can't perform research when the answer is dictated by personal prejudice. That goes against everything I've been taught."

I headed off Michaelson's explosion. She had just accused him of unprofessional behavior and quite possibly cooking his research data to fit his ill-conceived notions.

"What are your opinions on art? Modern art? Renaissance?"

"What are you blathering about, Thorne?" he demanded.

"Difference in opinion, in taste, in *belief*. You can never prove God doesn't exist."

"Of course not. Proving anything doesn't exist, except in a mathematical sense, is philosophically impossible. The only reason we do it in mathematics is by defining every element in the universe, then examining them individually.''

"You can't examine every element or combination of elements in this universe, can you?" I asked.

"Of course not. It's infinite," he said, as if lecturing a small child.

"Then credit me with my opinion that I can psychometrize. You don't have to believe it—but you can't disprove it, either."

"There's no evidence!" he howled.

"Your instruments show nothing. That doesn't mean nothing is there," I said. "You are apparently not measuring the right things. GSR and EEG and all the rest aren't responding, but I *hear* that knife shriek when I touch it. Whatever the cause, it is heavily charged with psychic energy and I tap into it."

I stared at the knife Barbara had placed on the table and shuddered. I couldn't see an aura around it, not unless I went into my trance, but I felt its enormous burden from across the room. It carried a potent charge of energy, and I acted as a lightning rod for it every time I touched it.

"You might be right, Thorne," said Michaelson. "Just because I've not recorded anything doesn't mean it isn't there." He smiled crookedly. "I'm not sure I know the units of measure for faith. How heavy is belief? Or does it come in kilowatts?"

"The knife," I insisted. "Was there *anything* unusual about it?"

Michaelson shook his head.

"I'm afraid we'll have to tell Cunningham this is a dead end. I don't want to touch the knife again. It overwhelms me."

"Have you got all the information you can from it?" asked Barbara.

"I doubt it. But ask a drowning man if he wants another glass of water. Sorting out the truth from the powerful hatred carried inside the crystal might be beyond my abilities."

"We've at least agreed on one point. Barbara's experiment is over," said Michaelson. "There's no point in pursuing it. It is only tying up valuable equipment and wasting our time."

"I want to continue, Doctor," I said.

"But, Thorne, you—" Michaelson's eyes widened in surprise.

"I volunteered to find out more of my talent. That still holds."

Michaelson turned to his graduate assistant. "It is both my right and duty to guide your research down productive avenues. I have several NMR projects you are well suited for. But as I said, I'll let you find another advisor if you insist on it."

"I want to continue with you." She stared him down. Michaelson was fuming and was about ready to boil over, but I guessed Barbara might be his best student and he was loathe to lose her like this.

"This goes against my better judgment. You can continue, but only for another week. You might have a better grasp of the problem and procedures than I do. But if there is no factual evidence by next Friday, we forget this nonsense."

I cleared my throat. This suited me fine. I had every confidence in Barbara's expertise and competence in designing an experiment to find the source of my power.

Michaelson spun and stormed from the laboratory. If he could have slammed the heavy metal door on its pneumatic closer, he would have.

"He thinks I am a faker."

"Don't be too hard on him, Peter," she said. "This is beyond his expertise. He knows everything there is about spins and magnetic moments. Is there a psychic spin? A quantum of mental energy? I just hope I can think of something to convince him to let us continue. I *know* this is a good experiment, Peter. You have the talents you claim. I *know* it."

"Thanks for the confidence," I said dryly. I stretched aching muscles and began pacing. There was nothing more to do here today. Investigating the knife scientifically had drawn a blank.

"Would you like to investigate a man who *is* a complete fraud? He's lived off gullible clients for years. It might give you some insight into designing a more comprehensive experiment—and one that will convince your advisor."

"Who's this?" Barbara asked.

"Damien Bishop," I said. "San Francisco's most notorious and best-paid astrologer."

"What's your interest in him?"

"The list of suspects Cunningham showed me," I said. "Damien Bishop was on it. Even if he doesn't have anything to do with Santorini's murder, exposing him would do everyone a big favor."

"I've read about Bishop," Barbara said, frowning as she tried to pick up the threads of the astrologer's fame. "You think he's a fraud?"

"Yes," I said softly. "I know he is." Other, older hurts rose to back my conviction. He *was* a fraud.

CHAPTER ELEVEN

"What did you say, Peter? You're mumbling," said Barbara Chan.

I craned my neck and stared up at the tall office building just down the street from the Transamerica spire. Damien Bishop kept house in fancy quarters—and I knew how he paid for it. We had crossed paths several times, and I found myself liking him less each time—if that was humanly possible. I know my talents and know which are only stage magic. When I perform, I make no bones about it being an act. Damien Bishop had built a career on people's gullibility. Even worse, he had a team of investigators prying into people's lives to find tidbits to spring on them, making his credibility all the greater.

If he had stopped there, I might have disliked him. He hadn't. He had done more, too much more.

The thoughts kept running over and over in my head. I barely heard what Barbara was saying.

"I exposed him, but he got out of it slicker than ice on glass," I muttered. I took a deep breath when I found Damien Bishop's name on the occupant listing sign. His was the only name in gold. The rest had to make do with the more usual white lettering.

"What are you talking about?" Barbara asked.

"The Challenger disaster. You remember it?"

"Of course. What's that got to do with Damien Bishop?"

"He tried to make it appear he had predicted it. He said Saturn's malign influence and Pluto's negative energy converged to destroy the shuttle. He claimed to have warned NASA a week earlier."

"Every dog has its day," Barbara said. "If you make enough wild guesses, one is bound to come true. Hadn't a respected engineer said there was one chance in ten of the Challenger blowing up?''

"Maybe. The point is, Bishop predicted it—and said he'd done it on a local talk show. He had the videotape.''

"The talk show's host could have verified it," said Barbara.

"She did. I dug around a bit and found that she and Damien Bishop were intimate.''

"Lovers?''

"What passes for it these days," I said with some scorn. "She lied—and the tape with its electronic time and date marking had been altered. He had someone do it for him. He's not smart enough to fake something that sophisticated.''

Barbara said something, but I was on a roll. The anger I felt toward Damien Bishop bubbled up. He was a fake, and I took that as a personal affront. Worse, he was partly responsible for the death of my wife.

"I found the technician who'd done it. He worked for a station down in San Jose. I have a complete write-up on how he duplicated the videotape and inserted a new date marker. Bishop had told him it was a joke. He didn't think anything about it.''

"Until Damien Bishop claimed that it was recorded before the Challenger's launch," Barbara finished for me. "He came to you? The video technician?''

"I found him. He hadn't even heard of Bishop's claims. He was more than happy to give me a sworn statement about what he had done and how he hadn't known how Bishop was going to use it.''

"I see you and the good astrologer go back a ways," Barbara said. "Have you had any contact with him recently?''

"None. Unless we just walk in, he won't see us if he knows who is calling on him." I had made up my mind to confront the crooked astrologer and watch him squirm. If he squirmed enough, he might even confess to a murder. He was fully capable of it if he thought Priscilla Santorini was going to unmask him for the fake that he is.

We entered the elevator and shot upward to the fortieth-floor offices of San Francisco's unofficial chief astrologer.

"Why didn't I see his claims about the Challenger explosion?" Barbara asked.

"He stopped just short of getting it on the national news. He knew what would happen if he came out and then I discredited him."

"He sounds like a treacherous snake," Barbara said. I didn't argue the point with her. I agreed. We stopped in front of elaborately wrought bronze doors. The signs of the zodiac curled around in a giant circle, the ram's horns of Aries forming the doorknobs. I had no trouble guessing Damien Bishop's sign. He advertised mercilessly.

Pretending I had his nose in my hand, I gave a ram's horn a savage twist and walked into the outer room. I hadn't been in this office before. Bishop's star had risen even more by the prosperity shown in the fixtures.

"Are they—" started Barbara. She bit back the question. I doubted Bishop wasted money on making the inner doors of real beaten gold leaf, though it was difficult to tell.

"Good afternoon," greeted a stately woman seated behind a desk devoid of all paper. I saw a clear glass plate on the writing surface and knew she had a computer hidden away out of sight. Knowing Bishop's predilection for quick answers to esoteric questions, she might have access to the fanciest, most complete database possible, perhaps even using a CD ROM player. I looked around but didn't see the computer. Considering how extensive this suite of offices was, Damien Bishop could hide a mainframe here and let visitors look for it for a week.

"I'm a colleague of Mr. Bishop's," I said. Using a bit of my finger dexterity, I produced a business card from thin air and handed it to her. I'll grant Bishop this: he hires the best. The woman never blinked when the card appeared. Only when it blazed away in a puff of flame and smoke did she react.

"I'm afraid you don't have an appointment, Mr. Thorne."

"I'm surprised Damien hasn't entered it on his log," I said. "He sees the future, doesn't he? He should have known I'd be along this afternoon."

"Really, sir," she said, smiling for the first time and

showing true amusement at my naivete. "Mr. Bishop concerns himself with only the most cosmic of events, not minor visitations by . . . stage magicians."

"In here, Peter," called Barbara. She went not to the doors of beaten gold but to a smaller door on the far side of the room. I glanced down and saw that a steady parade of feet had worn the carpet to this simpler entry.

"Wait, you can't barge in on him like that—"

She reached under the desk to touch a buzzer. I stopped her by slipping my hand under hers.

"He'll see us," I said softly. "Tell him it's about a mutual acquaintance. Priscilla Santorini."

"Ms. Santorini is no longer with us," she said in a distant voice. "It was such a tragedy."

"One I'm sure Damien will be more than happy to help us explore more fully." I motioned to Barbara to go ahead. She opened the door and roared into Damien Bishop's inner sanctum like a bull charging a matador. While this wasn't the best way of getting information from a person, I doubted we were going to get much more satisfaction from Bishop than seeing his startled expression when we presented ourselves.

By the time I got into Bishop's office, his hand was already on the intercom to demand of his usually efficient secretary the meaning of our intrusion. He didn't recognize Barbara. There was no time-delay when he saw me.

"Thorne!" How he managed to hiss out my name was a mystery known only to astrologers.

"Yes, Peter Thorne, Capricorn with Gemini ascendant," I said, enjoying the dark cloud of anger twisting his handsome face.

I looked around the office. For all the lavish splendor of statuary and flashy carpet and doors outside, he maintained an almost spartan simplicity within. The contrast doubtlessly appealed to his clients. The neutral gray rug was of good quality, as was the large wooden desk. I didn't recognize the type of wood, but I've seen bigger and more ornate ones in doctors' offices. Bishop had come half out of his leather swivel chair, of the type preferred by bank presidents. For all the simplicity of decoration in this office, he hadn't spared any expense to make himself comfortable.

Looking around, I saw a half dozen places where he might conceal recording devices, both video and audio. Bishop claimed the legal confidentiality of a lawyer but had the morals of a stepped-on pit viper. He wasn't above blackmailing his clients using information they'd given him—or which his teams of sleazy investigators had unearthed.

"What do you mean coming in here like this, Thorne?"

"I told your secretary we had something to discuss."

"We have nothing to talk over. Get out. And take your hussy with you." Bishop stared at Barbara for several silent seconds, then turned red in the face. It didn't go well with his normally pasty complexion.

"Mr. Thorne says you had business dealings several years ago." Barbara seemed to enjoy driving in the knife. Bishop turned even more livid.

"The Challenger explosion," Barbara went on. Bishop started to respond, then pulled back as if he had burned himself.

"Both of you, get out or I'll call the police."

"Call Lieutenant Cunningham, will you? He's with the California Highway Patrol. I know he's out in their Marin County station rather than here in the San Francisco office, but he might be able to help you find reasons to talk to us."

"You're a damned fraud!"

"Now isn't that the pot calling the kettle black?" I said. "Did Priscilla Santorini call you a fraud, too? Is that where you got that particular curse?" The expression on the astrologer's face was precious to me. He had cost me several bookings through his lies—and more. Giving Bishop a stroke now might compensate for the lost revenue. A little.

"Why do you keep mentioning her?" he said, settling into his posh leather chair. It seemed to swallow him as he tented his fingers under his chin and leaned back. He was regaining his composure.

"You were her astrologer," I said, taking a shot in the dark. "You were milking her for money. When she got tired of it and refused to pay any more extortion, you killed her.''

"Me, kill her? Don't be absurd,'' Bishop said. I saw the tiny twitches that would have sent Barbara's laboratory equipment into wild fits of electronic glee over the reaction. But was he lying?

"Mr. Thorne might be a little hasty in that accusation,'' Barbara said, taking the good guy role. I wanted to see him squirm some more. "But you must know you are a suspect. Lieutenant Cunningham told us you were her close friend. A very close friend.''

"Am I really under suspicion? I knew Priscilla, of course, but—'' He clamped his lips together firmly. For the briefest instant, his control had broken entirely and he'd spoken without thinking. I knew he had a ferocious temper. Getting him to confess to anything significant would have to be done by baiting him. But even if we did get any satisfaction from him, it wouldn't be admissible in court.

Still, if we could provide Cunningham enough evidence, he could home in on Bishop and not waste time on other suspects. Bishop was clever, but even a clever man committing murder makes a mistake somewhere.

"Perhaps I have it wrong. Maybe you weren't blackmailing her. Was she blackmailing you?'' I asked. "Had she caught you in another misadventure like the Challenger videotapes?''

"That was a misunderstanding. A reporter got the dates wrong, nothing more. You know that, Thorne,'' said Bishop. "Priscilla and I had a good relationship. She was interested in what the stars said about her and her finances.''

I snorted in contempt. Santorini had ended up just a bit poorer through her association with Damien Bishop—and the astrologer had come out just a bit richer. He wouldn't have tolerated her for an instant if it hadn't been that way.

"I know you for a liar and a cheat and an accessory to murder. You don't get the advice you sell your clients from the stars. You make it up to suit them, to fleece them.''

Damien Bishop leaned forward. He ignored Barbara completely, knowing I was his adversary. "This is getting tedious. Please state your business and then leave. I have appointments later today I must prepare for.''

I wanted Bishop on the defensive without time to compose himself.

''Why was she blackmailing you?'' I asked again. ''Isn't it usually the other way around in your field?''

''Priscilla and I were good, dear friends. I sometimes prepared horoscopes for her to aid in her investments. She was also interested in improving herself through New Age techniques. I helped her however I could.''

''I can go to the press with your being a suspect in her murder,'' I said. ''How's that going to look to your fancy clients? How many want to be seen going into an accused murderer's office?''

This panicked Damien Bishop. It was worth coming to his office to see the sheer terror flashing across his handsome Hollywood-surgeon-perfect face.

''I've got a syndicated television show starting next month,'' he said in a choked voice. ''They would cancel on me in a flash if you did that.'' Bishop puffed himself up. ''I'll sue you if you cause me to lose that show.''

''Peter might not have to make the accusation,'' Barbara said coolly. I admired her more every minute. She had come to my rescue. ''So sue me. I'm a college student. Just rolling in money. Take everything I have—if you can win in court. Truth is always a perfect defense. You can't use your charts to predict how a jury is going to rule.''

Bishop was no fool. He had spent most of his life conning people, but in court he'd be against a lovely woman who might be his match on the stand. On such things were juries swayed. It was sexist and against the principles of American jurisprudence, but it was also a cold, hard fact.

''Perhaps we can come to some financial agreement. You might need a grant to conduct research. I have many well-off patrons inclined to donate to the sciences.''

''I wouldn't touch your bribe money with a pair of laboratory tongs,'' Barbara said.

''I'll have you thrown out of whatever pathetic school you're at. I'll—''

Bishop continued his tirade against Barbara. I knew we'd

learn nothing from him now by further questioning. My mind began to drift, to float like a leaf on a gentle wind. I forced myself to breathe slowly, deeply. Mind-expanding oxygen entered my brain and added to a sense of well-being, of peace and serenity in a pool of inky blackness and insecurity. Everything but knowledge of the slow internal rhythm of my body vanished and the pulsating aura of objects around me began to deepen in hue and become visible to my inner eye.

Barely hearing Bishop and Barbara arguing, I leaned forward and put my hands on a file folder at the side of the desk. The instant I touched it, Bishop reacted as if I'd scalded him.

He jerked the folder away and stuffed it into his top desk drawer. The anger mounted to thunderstorm proportions.

"Get the hell out of my office," he yelled.

The sudden movement broke my trance. I blinked and smiled crookedly, only slightly aware of my surroundings. It took several seconds to recuperate.

"You don't have to answer our questions about your relationship with the deceased," I said. "You might not even have to answer Lieutenant Cunningham's. But will the Pentagon understand?"

With that I spun and walked out, leaving a sputtering astrologer behind. Barbara trailed behind, asking what I'd meant.

The brief psychometric flash I had received from the manila folder showed military troop movements and the huge expanse of the Pentagon and little else. I shrugged off Barbara's questions. I couldn't answer them.

But Damien Bishop might later.

CHAPTER TWELVE

"I want him as much now as I did earlier," I said with feeling. Barbara looked at me curiously. My vehemence came from something more than the desire of an academic who wants only to blow away the fogs of ignorance. I didn't know if Barbara could understand. Her own feelings seemed far more moderate than mine.

"Well?" she prompted. "What did we find out? Really?"

"You know it's not just intellectual honesty, don't you?" I heaved a sigh and looked upward toward Damien Bishop's fortieth-story office. "It's the money he makes from bilking the public. There's nothing honest about him."

"So he's a slimy snake. It doesn't take an Einstein to figure that out. But this is more than a moral issue with you, Peter. You lost money to a psychic?"

"No." The bitterness burned me.

"You don't have to tell me."

"The fake psychic healers. The ones who give bad advice. The ones who kill by keeping their victims away from legitimate doctors by assuring them everything is all right."

"Someone close to you died because of a psychic healer?"

"My wife." I swallowed hard. "She died of cancer five years ago. It might not have been curable—but in the hands of a . . . a charlatan, she died as surely as if he had driven a knife into her heart."

"There's more. I hear it when you talk about Damien Bishop. I have no liking for the man. I certainly have no respect, even before I learned of his trick with the video-tape after the Challenger explosion."

"He and the healer were in league. My wife paid him huge amounts of money to cast her horoscope. He told her she would live a long, fulfilling life if she trusted her closest advisors. She took that to mean the woman 'curing' her by laying on of hands. Marla Wise performed psychic surgery and my wife thought she was cured. She never once mentioned going to her. I thought she was seeing a real doctor. Heaven knew it was expensive enough. I had to work two jobs to make ends meet.''

Barbara nodded but thankfully said nothing. I thought I had gotten over the hurt. I was wrong. Over the years, I had watched dozens of such performances. The sleight-of-hand performed rivalled my own. A psychic surgeon rubbed the patient's belly with an open palm, then doubled up fingers and ''psychically'' and dramatically drew forth a tumor. It was usually a chicken gizzard or other viscera cleverly produced without incision.

Her dark eyes locked on mine and filled with tears. Reading Barbara's expression proved impossible. I reached to stop her as she turned and hurried off, then decided against it. She was upset because I was upset. I remembered what I had psychometrically learned of her past and wondered if I had accidentally opened an old wound in her, too. Her parents had died, but I had no idea how.

Barbara turned the corner and vanished, but I knew I'd see her again. If she hadn't got in touch with me in a day or two, I'd call her. Then we could work out our mutual hurt. I had been wrong to dump so much on her like this.

I walked along the street, found Montgomery and began drifting down it without any real destination in mind. The meeting with Damien Bishop had whetted my taste for finding the reason Priscilla Santorini had died—and how the crystal knife had become so potently charged. It was none of my business. Lieutenant Cunningham and the California Highway Patrol were eminently more qualified to investigate this murder. Santorini was nothing to me. I had barely heard the name before being handed the quartz knife used to kill her.

As I thought of that knife, and Bishop, I knew I wasn't going to stop poking around. Smiling, decision made, I walked with more determination. There were other names on Cunningham's list of suspects. I found the office building housing a number of small brokerage houses.

Bishop was a closed door—for the moment. Others on Cunningham's list might be more open. Benjamin Larson had been Priscilla Santorini's financial manager. What I might be able to find out from him was unclear. I'd never know, though, until I asked.

The building where Larson's firm was located dated back to just after the 1906 earthquake and fire. The building pleased me with its ornate decoration and stolid appearance. I stopped for a moment and placed my hands against its cool stone exterior. Soothing waves passed through me, as much from psychometrizing as from the physical sensation of smoothness. More composed, I went inside to the bank of four rickety elevators.

Luckily, they were not antique in operation. After an unsettling grinding and jostling, the cage lifted smoothly for the eighth floor. I got out of the elevator and glanced out a window down Montgomery. From this height the trolleys sparked along their wires and looked like giant electric bugs. The pit leading to the BART sucked in hundreds of people, the vortex of pedestrians vanishing and none surfacing. I waited a few minutes until a pair of lonesome stragglers made their way up from the depths of the subway, reassuring me that this wasn't some unknown sinkhole for humanity.

I found Larson's office easily. The young, attractive receptionist smiled mechanically at me, her thoughts a thousand miles away.

"Benjamin Larson, please," I said.

"He's in conference," she lied automatically. "May I take your name and have him call you later in the day?"

"It's about Priscilla Santorini's account. The one he mismanaged."

I expected a burst of outrage, then a threat to be ejected from the office if I didn't leave voluntarily. To my surprise, the woman's eyes turned into bright blue saucers and she stammered something I couldn't catch. I realized the words hadn't been directed at me when a distinguished, gray-haired man burst from an office. The panicked expression faded when he saw me. Whoever he had anticipated, I wasn't it.

"What is this?" he demanded.

"Mr. Benjamin Larson?"

"Of course I am. I'm senior partner in this firm. What's the meaning of your accusations? Who *are* you? Show me your credentials."

"I'm not from the SEC," I said. "I'm working with Lieutenant Cunningham on Ms. Santorini's murder case."

The relief flowed over Benjamin Larson's face like a wave across the choppy ocean.

"In what capacity? You haven't shown any credentials."

"I was a . . . friend," I said. "A recent acquaintance, but she spoke highly of you."

"Then what—" Benjamin Larson cut off his question. "Come in, please. I didn't catch your name."

"Peter Thorne," I said, pushing past him into the office. He was a man of traditional tastes, but I'd guessed as much from his pinstripe three-piece suit and black wing-tip shoes. The office reflected a firm attachment to more distant times. The office and building had much in common as far as age went. Heavy leather furniture sat around the perimeter of the room. A banker's light with a green plastic shade provided the only illumination on the desk. Roller blinds and drapes of an antique pattern shut out too much of the light for my taste.

"There, Mr. Thorne. Please be seated."

Benjamin Larson went around the desk and pulled the comfortable chair under him. He sat with a hesitation that made me wonder about infirmity. It might have been nothing more than hemorrhoids or it could have been a faulty hip. Benjamin Larson was getting to the age where joints wore out. It was hard putting him in Priscilla Santorini's jet set gaggle of friends.

"What was this about, uh, misconduct?" he asked tentatively.

"Nothing much. It was just that Priscilla mentioned that she and you had, shall we say, skirted the law on a deal or two."

"Priscilla never had a head for business," Larson said. "Things about the financial world always struck her as illegal or immoral. That's why I handled all her business affairs."

"If not her other ones," I said dryly.

"Have you gained entry to my office through misleading statements, Mr. Thorne?"

I didn't know the proper questions to ask of Benjamin Larson. He panicked too easily when he had thought I was with the Securities and Exchange Commission. His dealings with Santorini had not been of the purest quality, I guessed. I took a shot at what their relationship might have been.

"How many times did she give you insider information she'd weaseled out of her lovers?"

Larson stiffened and stared at me with a look so hot that it might have burned into my soul.

"I do not know what you mean. I resent these insinuations. And I doubt you were any friend of Priscilla's."

"I was," I lied. "I was an advisor on New Age matters."

"She didn't need one. She was well read on the subject. And she always found her own crystals. Heaven alone knows I never believed in that claptrap, but that wasn't my . . . duty. I invested for her and kept her financially sound."

"You would have steered her away from perfecting her spirit?" I asked.

"Of course not. I know something about New Age philosophy. Rebirthing is a part of it and Priscilla was interested in attaining a higher plateau of existence. I simply mean that it is not my path. She did as she chose."

A hint of bitterness tinged Larson's voice. I reached out and touched his desk set. The pen had been laid down beside a stack of papers he had been working on when I interrupted him. The pencil remained in the polished walnut base. I let myself drift and entered a light trance. It was difficult to do while carrying on a conversation. My voice slowed and deepened, as if dipped in molasses, and I experienced a lethargy.

The desk set's aura wavered, turning green and yellow and blue, then warming. Images came and voices spoke and I tasted and smelled and pieced together random impressions.

"You've had the set for some time," I said. "Priscilla gave it to you."

Larson jerked as if I'd stuck him with a needle.

"She did. In appreciation for my years of service."

"Of servicing her," I said.

"I beg your pardon, sir!"

"You were intimate with her. Many times." The rush of other information overwhelmed me and I came out of the light trance state. Santorini had used him, but I hadn't been able to get a sense of how. Perhaps sex for her was nothing more than a way of keeping a valued employee in line. For Larson it had been more. That much was etched on his wrinkled face.

"You're trying to blackmail me. It won't work, Thorne. I didn't kill her and have no idea who did. Now get the hell out of here."

I turned and stared at the computer sitting in a corner of the room. The monitor's green screen winked and glowed with the steady flow of numbers across it. The information it gave up so easily meant nothing to me, but it must to Larson.

"Stock information," I muttered, more to myself than to him. "Insider information gathered during pillow talk."

"Get out or I'll call the police."

I rose and left without another word. I had a peek into Benjamin Larson's life and relationship with Priscilla Santorini, but it didn't satisfy me. I had missed so much. I needed more. A man had killed Santorini, but I got no feeling that Larson had been the one. In his way, he still loved her.

As I got into the elevator, a woman was leaving. She turned away from me. Our shoulders brushed and her handbag got tangled as I reached out to hold open the door. She jerked away, head averted so I couldn't see her face.

I got in the elevator and let the door shut. A wave of sensation passed through me. The brief touch with the woman's purse had sparked in me a moment of . . . fear.

Confusion made me clumsy. I tried unsuccessfully to stop the elevator and return to Benjamin Larson's floor.

The elevator reached the second floor before I got it stopped and turned around.

Impatiently, I tapped my foot until the cage reached the eighth floor again. I rushed into Larson's office. I just glanced at his secretary. The woman lay slumped forward. It didn't take a doctor to realize she had been killed.

I flung open the door to Larson's office, not knowing what I'd find, but expecting the worst. His chair was turned around. He couldn't be looking out the window; the blinds were still drawn. I skirted the desk and came around the chair.

My stomach began to churn when I saw Larson's open, sightless eyes. Just below his chin protruded the razor-edge of a Japanese throwing star, a *shuriken*.

I rushed back to the hall and looked up and down. The woman wasn't in sight. She might have taken one of the other elevators or even the stairway to ground level. However she vanished, she had committed a double murder, then left before I could travel back up in the elevator.

Willie Worthington had to be contacted. I went back into Benjamin Larson's silent office to phone him.

CHAPTER THIRTEEN

"Ten seconds, max."

"What?" I hadn't been paying any attention to Worthington's mumbled comments. For the first time in several minutes, I came out of my daze and stared at him.

"Well planned," he said, chewing on his yellow pencil. "Ten seconds. That's all it took for the murders. I got it figured this way. The killer steps into the outer office. The secretary looks up. Whish! A star in her throat. She falls forward. Then the killer comes in here. Whish! The second star gets Larson just under the jaw, severing his carotid. He falls back and the chair swivels around under his weight."

"Which is how I found him," I concluded.

"Looks like," said Worthington. "Slick killings. A real pro did it." He looked at me until I squirmed.

"I didn't see anyone, except the woman I bumped into."

"Could have been done by a woman, but she'd have to have quite an arm. The ME says the throwing stars about took their heads off. Sharp edges, sure, but one hell of a lot of power behind the throw." Worthington looked at me again, his head cocked to one side.

"I felt something," I said, paying scant attention to him. "When I brushed against the woman's purse, I felt something unsettling."

"Like what? That she was the one who croaked these two?"

"Possibly. There was something wrong, and I can't put my finger on it. She had a strong presence—the bag did."

"Might have been the throwing stars," guessed Worthington.

"May I touch one?" He handed me a bagged *shuriken*, the one that had snuffed out Benjamin Larson's life. Holding only the plastic, I settled my thoughts the best I could.

My hand reached out and rested on the deadly steel device inside.

Trembling, I dropped the bag to Larson's desk.

"So? Whodunnit, Sherlock?"

"Willie, it—it's frightening. I've never sensed anything like it. A man killed Larson."

"So it's not the broad you ran into on the elevator, unless the guy was in drag."

"It was a woman," I said, sure of myself on this point. "And there's something very similar to Priscilla Santorini's killing. The unchecked violence wasn't here. This was a cold-blooded killing, but the same man might have done it."

"Get me something I can take to court. Not the woman, but we're going to start looking for her. She might have seen the murderer coming out. There wasn't much time between you leaving and finding the stiffs."

"No," I said, distracted. I felt a victim of sensory overload. There were so many similarities to the *feel* of the killers, yet there were differences, too. Larson had died because of something he knew. Santorini died because of a jilted lover. The first was business; Santorini's death had been intensely personal.

"You look like shit. Go on home. I'll be in touch," Worthington said. "I won't even offer to buy you lunch."

"Thank heavens for small favors," I said, grinning weakly.

"Wish I'd get a break," Worthington said, sighing like a fumarole. "I got to go to Cunningham with this. Larson was a suspect on his list. Now we got to share evidence. Talk about bad luck. CHPs, bah."

I left, my head still spinning from the murders. The *shuriken* had been wielded by an expert who knew exactly what he wanted to do. Ten seconds between entry and death—that was what Worthington said. I should have been able to do more. If only my talent let me see, really see!

I wandered the downtown area for a while, then sat on a bench in Union Square alternately staring down Maiden Lane at the shoppers and people eating at the open-air cafes and watching the sea gulls swooping on them for a quick meal. The sun melted over me, warm and sensuous, and allowed me to put my mind in neutral. I allowed random impressions to flutter by.

I didn't know Priscilla Santorini and, if it came down to putting value judgments on unknown and very dead people, I probably wouldn't have liked her had I known her. Damien Bishop had been an intimate of hers. He was a man who made his fortune off the fears and weakness of others. Benjamin Larson might not be any better, but he had been eliminated as a suspect. The brief psychometry I had done in his office had left me tired and confused but sure he had nothing to do with Santorini's killing.

The more I thought about it, the more certain I became that the broker and the socialite shared more than a bed—they shared a killer.

I sighed. This was none of my business. I was a stage magician by profession and had a gig coming up in less than two weeks to prepare for. Exercise to keep in trim was needed. I needed to find a new assistant since my last one had gotten pregnant and moved to Oregon with her boyfriend.

It was none of my business—but the quartz knife kept returning to haunt me. I'd never be able to forget the hideous screams it emitted when I touched it. Just being near it upset me unduly. Never had I faced such a potent relic before. Perhaps that more than anything else drew me.

I wasn't a devout believer in the New Age philosophy of rebirth, though I shared some of the belief of human perfection. That put me at odds with most Christians, but it felt right.

It would also feel right to know who had killed Priscilla Santorini. And Benjamin Larson.

I heaved to my feet and turned down Grant Avenue and went to Market, not knowing where I went. Before long I realized I had curled around and had come back to Powell. I plugged my five-dollar bill into the ticket machine, got change and a green ticket for the cable car. Luckily, the cable car was almost empty between rushes of tourists and commuters.

I rode to the top of California, jumped off and caught the Mason Street car. At the foot of the hill, I wended my way through to the seamy section of the world. In many ways, the North Beach area was even more exotic and alien than Chinatown.

The list of suspects Cunningham had flashed in front of me burned like fire in my brain. I'd spoken with two of the men. The third name on the list was the pivotal one for my involvement. If Willie Worthington hadn't asked me to check into this, I'd never have heard the knife's death cry close up.

Steve Hackett was a curious choice to be friends with a society doyenne—except for the cocaine I'd sensed in her bedroom. Hackett had a reputation among the nightclub entertainers I knew as always having just the right illicit substance at just the right price.

The numerous gay clubs and leather bars made me uneasy. I forced it away. My sexual preferences were well rooted rather than ambiguous, and I knew the male role fit me comfortably. Ignoring the come-ons was the least of my problems here. There were as many junkies likely to bash me over the head for a few dollars and a quick fix as they were to proposition me. I had come from the section of town where everyone looked like Ted Bundy to the part where everyone looked like Charles Manson.

I stopped and thought about how to find Hackett and banish the prejudicial dread bothering me. Finding an unoccupied corner with a decently flat concrete bench wasn't hard. I took a few coins from my pocket and began running them up and down my fingers, simple exercises to improve dexterity.

Within minutes, I had a small but appreciative crowd who had nothing better to do while waiting for a bus. From this start, I produced a few cards from inner pockets and started into a three-card monte routine. The cards scraped and hissed on the seat of the bench. If anything, this added to the appeal.

"Want to place a wager on where the queen is?" I asked a bystander, showing the queen of diamonds between two deuces.

Someone in the crowd guffawed and said, "Finding a queen around here is easy. Finding a spade queen ain't hard, either."

The crowd laughed nervously. I started the shuffle,

moving the cards in and out, in and out until the queen vanished in the scurrying back and forth.

"What's the bet?" asked a smallish man who looked more like a weasel than a human. His eyes darted to and fro and never lighted on anything. From the poor cut of his tattered clothes and his alienation from soap, I recognized in him someone who might furnish me with the information I needed.

"Make it easy on yourself," I said, showing the edge of the queen and bending the card slightly. The deuces remained unscathed; the queen of diamonds was marked. I acted as if I hadn't noticed it.

"A dollar," he said, going along with me. I let him win the first two for a dollar. In this day and age it amazes me there are people who don't understand this simple variation on the shell game.

"Want to make it five?" I asked.

"Sure." He looked back and forth furtively, as if he was on the lookout for someone.

"Is that a policeman coming?" I asked. My mark almost bolted. I knew I had the right man. "Guess not," I said before he could run. "It must have been a soldier in uniform." I laid out the cards in front of me, the buckled one in the center.

"Five?"

"Why not?" I said.

He won easily.

"Let's make it ten," I said. "You've already got seven of my dollars. Give me a chance to get it back. You can't be this lucky all the time."

"Not luck," he said. "I got good eyes."

"Let's check that out." I ran the cards from side to side and left the buckled one in the center.

"It's the center one," he said. He stopped me before I could turn it over and show that it wasn't the queen. "It's got to be the queen if the other two aren't." He reached out and flipped over the two side cards. The deuces showed up. He smiled crookedly and grabbed for the ten-dollar bill I'd placed on the ground beside the cards.

I grabbed his wrist. We both stood. The crowd sensed trouble brewing and backed off to watch. They might even be putting down bets on the outcome. It was that kind of neighborhood.

"I won fair and square, unless that ain't a queen in the center," he said.

"What makes you think I'm cheating?" I bent forward and flipped over the middle card. It was the queen. The man's dark eyes widened in surprise. The usual hustle is to substitute another deuce for the bent queen.

"I don't understand," he said.

"I was looking for you," I said. He started to bolt again. I stopped him. "I want some information—and am willing to pay for it."

"I don't know nothing."

"Steve Hackett. Where do I find him?"

He licked his lips. "Anybody could tell you that. Why me?"

"You're here—and you already have seventeen dollars toward me paying for the information."

"I won that fair," he whined.

"I'll give you twenty for the information." I reached into my pocket and pulled out a crumpled bill. The sight of Andy Jackson loosened his tongue.

"He's over at the Charade. A bar two blocks down and one toward the Bay. Gimme." He snatched at the twenty and ran. I let him go. The crowd around us had dissipated, the cheap drifters and con artists gone with the gawkers. I took the man's wallet out of my pocket and rifled through it. Besides the twenty I'd given back to him, he had a fifty and seven different IDs. From my other pocket I took out the money he'd won and stuffed into his pants pocket. Being a pick pocket isn't difficult when the victim is already distracted.

I started walking toward the Charade, thinking how I'd approach Hackett. The way the grapevine worked, he already knew someone was looking for him.

Two blocks down the street I stopped to watch a juggler sweating to keep a bowling ball, a chair and a lighted torch in a stack. He did a good job.

"Catch," I said when he had lowered the bowling bowl to the ground. The small green wad arched up and down into his capable hand. It took him a couple seconds to unfold it.

"Thanks, mister. Here's a real patron of the arts, friends!" he cried, showing the fifty I'd given him. I smiled and went on. However the weasel had come by the money, it wasn't likely to be honest. The juggler was good and deserved encouragement. Who knows, one day he might make it to the level of the Flying Karamazov Brothers.

The Charade had a sign badly in need of paint. A few hours later, it would show at least a dozen burned-out bulbs on its sign. Right now, the afternoon sun simply showed it for a tawdry place. The inside was no better. Stale beer and sour vomit tore at my nostrils. I have to keep telling myself people actually come to dives like this to get drunk.

Around the walls were gaudily painted ceramic masks, the kind sold on Bourbon Street in New Orleans for Mardi Gras celebrants. Paint and the walls themselves were distant relatives. The linoleum floor had pieces knocked out of it and dirt had accumulated. It made me feel unclean just walking across it.

Steve Hackett sat at a back table, hunched over a watery drink. Never was a man so out of place. The Charade was tacky; Steve Hackett wore a fifteen-hundred-dollar custom-tailored silk suit, the jacket hanging over the back of a chair beside him. From the way his belt was cinched up around his waist, he had lost a considerable amount of weight recently and hadn't let anyone retailor the pants. His hair, while expertly cut, was tousled, as if he hadn't combed it recently. He made intricate notations on a sheet of paper, which disappeared faster than I could have done with my own sleight-of-hand.

"What do you want?" he demanded. He frowned, trying to place me. We had never met, but I'm sure he had been in a few clubs where I'd performed. I raked up old memories and found a more personal nexus.

"We were both at Elizabeth Jennings' party six months ago," I said in way of introduction.

"I don't know—yeah, I know you. You're a magician."

"Peter Thorne," I furnished. There wasn't any need for him to strain for the name.

"Yeah, right." He rocked back and crossed his arms over his chest, saying nothing.

"I need some . . . information," I said.

"I don't know anything." Something about Hackett bothered me. His abrupt, rude manner wasn't what put me off. There was something more about him that worked to the core of my soul. I didn't know if I should fear him or feel sorry for him.

Worthington wanted to tie drug-dealing charges on him. I wondered why that was a problem. Hackett didn't seem the kind to be too careful about his dealings. What struck me as truly odd was the notion of him being Priscilla Santorini's supplier. A woman of her social strata could have found sources of drugs closer to her station. Then I remembered her bondage fetish. She had a taste for the low, the bizarre. Why not a dealer of Hackett's caliber?

"How much did Priscilla Santorini buy from you?"

His face melted and his expression turned neutral. I vowed to never play cards with him. He had the most unreadable countenance of anyone I'd come across in a long while.

"Too bad about her getting wasted like that," Hackett said in a flat voice. "I read about it. She was a foxy one, you know?"

I knew nothing about interrogation techniques. Whatever there was to be found out from Steve Hackett was better left to professionals. Cunningham could find Steve Hackett with no problem; Willie Worthington knew about him, too. After Benjamin Larson's death, Hackett might vault to the tops of both their wanted lists.

"She was that," I answered. "Buy you a drink? Or have you had enough?" I looked at the half dozen wet rings on the table, mostly fresh. If Hackett had been the one producing them, he had been here for some time—which eliminated him as a suspect in Larson's murder.

"I'm fine," he said in a monotone. "I got reports to work on. If there's nothing I can do for you, and there isn't, why don't you push off? I'll catch your act, and maybe we can socialize then."

"Sorry to have taken up your time," I said, sticking out my hand to shake. He recoiled as if I'd struck him. Feeling foolish, I rose. Hackett slipped out from behind the table. As he did, his expensive jacket fell to the floor.

"Let me get it," I said, being nearer the coat. I touched the silk collar and recoiled. A polar chill raced through me and I almost fainted. Deathly white enveloped me. Icicles poked into my gut and refused to leave. The coat slipped from my nerveless fingers. Steve Hackett caught it before it hit the floor again.

"You all right, Thorne? You don't look so good."

I stared at him. "Are *you* all right?"

A frightened look crossed his passive face. He ran from the Charade. I caught a glint of sunlight off his shiny jacket as he turned and raced off in the direction of Coit Tower.

CHAPTER FOURTEEN

I sat in the Hall of Justice waiting for Willie Worthington to finish with a distraught woman in his office. From my vantage on the hard bench next to the coffee machine, I watched as the woman gestured wildly. Once she tipped over Worthington's cup. He didn't even move to clean up the spill. His eyes fixed firmly on her, as if she had become the center of his universe.

Their words were muffled by the glass partition between us. I concentrated, heard only snippets, then relaxed. Nothing of interest to me went on in the detective's office. I closed my eyes and started breathing deeply, slowly, letting the details of Priscilla Santorini's death float like cork on the surface of my mind.

Nothing useful bobbed up. Too many waves created an unclear picture of what really came to the surface. Benjamin Larson muddied the waters, but I had already lumped his death with Santorini's. Find one's murderer, get the other's in one fell swoop. Steve Hackett was there, veiled in dark mist. But others came and went through the picture, such as Damien Bishop. I had hoped to use my psychometric powers to come to a speedy conclusion, but the knife, the damnable crystal knife obscured everything.

I winced as I mentally experienced its shrill, haunting scream. The crystal blade had been too firmly imprinted with hatred and the victim's vanishing life force for good psychometrizing.

Forcing the ringing echoes of death from my mind did little to give me peace. Under this layer of pain and death lay another.

The shovel. The one Barbara had said was a control. The blackness soared above me, then came crashing down with the force of a pile driver. I gasped for air. My shoulder jerked and twitched.

"Should I throw water on you?" came the faint words.
I forced open my eyes. Worthington stared at me, a
mixture of concern and disgust on his face. He wasn't sure
if I was having a seizure or had taken some fancy new
designer drug.

"I'm not inclined to do dope," I told him.

"Didn't think you were," he said. "It's hard to tell
these days." He shrugged eloquently, as if adding, "You
know how it is with you show biz people."

Two quick, short breaths cleared most of the imagery
from my head. I swiped at the sweat dripping down my
temples. Keeping a rein on my mental wanderings would
have to take a higher priority in the future. Looking ill—
or on drugs—would do nothing for my star billing.

"What did you want to see me about? I read over your
statement on the Larson thing and it looks good." Worthington continued to study me, as if he expected me to turn
into a butterfly and flutter off.

"You asked me to get a line on Steve Hackett. I did."

"Come on into the pigsty," he said, motioning vaguely
toward his office. Worthington looked around the room.
"I'm sure you can leave these rocket scientists behind."

A uniformed sergeant reading a comic book at a nearby
desk looked up and shot Worthington a finger. Worthington
took no notice of it, if he even saw it. The sergeant went
back to his *Dark Knight* and I went into Worthington's office.

"I'd offer you some coffee, but the cup's broken." He
kicked the pieces of the fallen mug under his desk. "Got
to get a new one. That one was dirty."

Settling gingerly into his chair, I sensed a flash of anger.
The woman who had been here before me had imprinted
a large, if evanescent, emotional burst on the chair.

"Her daughter?" I asked.

Before he had wondered if I was on drugs. Now he
looked at me as if he knew I was. He ran his hands through
his hair in a way showing extreme irritation.

"The old lady thinks her girl's out hooking in the Ten-
derloin. I tried to tell her this was homicide. How the hell
she got past Rico or Pleasance outside is beyond me. She
really bent my ear about runaways and how nobody cares.
The same old story. I sent her over to Missing Persons."

"They won't look," I said.

"Why should they? They've got a lifetime of work ahead of them now without going after an eighteen-year-old. Hell, the kid's no kid. That's adult. She can vote."

"Her mother's still worried," I said softly.

"So you go comfort her," snapped Worthington. "This hasn't been a good day. I got three—count 'em, three— new cases this morning. That's not counting the Larson mess you dumped on me yesterday. You want to earn some points here, you solve those crimes. Do that and I'll go ringing doorbells to find the old lady's kid."

"You wanted to know about Steve Hackett," I said. Worthington is usually calm and orderly when it comes to his work. It didn't take a psychologist to see he was under considerable pressure. For my own part, I was feeling the strain, too. When I told him what little I had found out about Steve Hackett, my obligation would end. I could think about my opening in two weeks and forget playing detective, a role less to my liking with every passing minute.

"So what did you find out about him?"

"He's a drug dealer. I suspect his income is mostly from cocaine."

"Yeah, what else?" Worthington sounded tired rather than angry and frustrated now. I wasn't sure this was any improvement.

"What else did you want to know about him?" I remembered the blackness surrounding the man, but I still couldn't put into words its cause.

"There have been a series of drug-related murders in the past four months. Hackett is like the hub of a huge, illicit wheel. Everything turns around him, but there don't seem to be any spokes, if you catch my drift."

"There's a darkness about him," I muttered.

"How's that?" Worthington pushed himself erect in his chair and leaned forward, forearms on the edge of his desk. His eyes glowed with an intensity bordering on fever.

"He dropped his coat, and I picked it up for him. That brief touch. The darkness. It was an inky curtain. I've never seen anything quite like it."

"Did you shake hands with him?"

"No." I stared at Worthington. He'd known the answer. "Why do you ask?"

"He's a weird duck. Never lets anyone touch him."

"The darkness might have something to do with Priscilla Santorini's death," I said.

"You think so?"

I shook my head. The blackness told of death but carried none of the stark violence and soul-tearing passion locked in the crystal knife.

"You think it could be that Hackett knows the nose candy he puts out on the street is killing people? Maybe kids?" Worthington kept digging, but none of his suggestions rang with the silver peal of truth.

"I think he's involved with death. He might use his own coke." Even this didn't sound right to me. Worse, it didn't *feel* right. In spite of the torment it would have caused me, I wished I had been able to get a clearer reading on Steve Hackett.

"Hell, yes, he's involved with death. The drug-related ones. I don't think he's got the guts to do the murdering himself, but he knows plenty of people who could. He's the state's star witness, if we can get to him." Worthington leaned back, his eyes still on me. I felt like dinner for a large raptor.

"Are you going to speak with Cunningham?" I asked.

"Hackett's not his prime suspect, is he? I didn't think so. No, Hackett's ass is going to be mine. I don't think even the California Highway Patrol wants to pin a bad rap on Hackett to clear its books."

"A man did kill Santorini. It might have been Hackett."

"But you don't think so," Worthington pressed. "No, I see by your expression you don't. This crazy blackness isn't the right blackness for you."

"No, it isn't," I said, rising.

Worthington had solidified my thoughts about Steve Hackett. The cocaine dealer might be many things, he might be involved in the drug deaths Worthington was investigating, but Hackett had not killed Priscilla Santorini. The harmonics were all wrong for that.

CHAPTER FIFTEEN

I kept going over what Willie Worthington had said—and what he hadn't said. He was reporting everything I'd told him to Cunningham, with some reluctance. If it hadn't been for the link between Larson and Santorini, there would have been no contact. There wasn't any love lost between the SFPD and the California Highway Patrol. In the strictest sense, Worthington didn't have anything important to pass along since I had uncovered nothing definite about Hackett. The vague notion of blackness wrapping the man could mean anything. It certainly lacked the solidity needed to take him to court for murder, or drug dealing or much of anything except frequenting sleazy bars.

I walked aimlessly, letting the chilly breeze off the Bay keep me on edge physically if not mentally. The more I thought about the murders, the deeper into the psychic maze I felt drawn. Living with the echoes of the knife wouldn't be easy.

I damned Worthington and Cunningham and even Priscilla Santorini and Benjamin Larson for dying. I didn't need this kind of frustration. Everyone who even halfway believed I had any skill looked on it as a trick, something akin to pulling coins from behind the ear of a small boy. Such a trick was performed quickly and even more quickly forgotten.

The agonized cries locked within the crystal structure of the quartz blade continued to blast through my skull. In the physical world, echoes die over time and distance. It didn't work like that on a psychic plane, much to my regret.

My steps turned uphill. I crossed Powell, going up a steep incline before I realized how long I had been walking. Stopping to consider my options, I knew there wouldn't be any relief for me until Santorini's murderer was brought to justice. Even then, the crystal blade might haunt my dreams—and waking hours—for a long, long time.

I ducked into a small cafe on Union, found the pay phone and rustled through the pages until I found the listing for Benjamin Larson. Whatever caused my feet to move in this direction had left me less than a half mile from his home. Who stayed at home during the day? Finding out would keep me busy for a while longer.

The wind picked up and added a steel edge as I made my way up the slope toward Larson's fashionable address. When I stopped in front of Larson's house, I wondered just how much of the mortgage payment came from Priscilla Santorini's fees. Guesses about the size of the house made me wonder if Larson had bivouacked an army on the grounds—or inside.

Passing the iron gates and walking up the drive sent shivers along my spine. Most people work on first impressions, whether they admit it or not. Psychometry gives me a deeper understanding to form my opinions, but they usually aren't any different from the brief glance and knowledge you like or hate someone. Larson's house sucked out the warmth from my body and made me realize how little love there was in the world.

At the front door, complete with beveled, etched glass and polished wood equal to a month's salary for most people, this impression hit me even harder. Coldness. Aloofness. Don't touch, stay back.

"Yes?" The woman who answered the door was dressed as if she was ready to go out on the town. Her graying hair was whirled into an elaborate hairdo. Closer examination showed that it wasn't exactly gray. Rather, it had been frosted in a style I hadn't seen in years. Her dress, although expensive, was subtly deviant from the current *haute couture*. She seemed trapped in a time warp five years old.

"My name is Peter Thorne," I said, wondering how to approach her.

"Is it about my husband?"

"You're Mrs. Larson?"

"I am Estelle Larson," she said cautiously. "Are you with the police? They had men here all yesterday afternoon. I don't think they learned anything."

"No, Mrs. Larson, I'm not a policeman." Explaining just what the hell I was doing baffled me for a moment. Truth was usually the best solution in such cases, though it might get the door slammed in my face. "I'm sorry about your husband's death. I think it might be linked with Priscilla Santorini's murder."

Estelle Larson didn't need to say a word. I read the surprise on her face, followed by a look of distaste that, if put into words, would have been "that bitch!"

"You can call Detective Worthington of the SFPD or Lieutenant Cunningham of the California Highway Patrol. Either will vouch for me." I didn't add that neither would approve of this interrogation.

"I don't understand. What is . . . was your relationship with that woman?" The words burned Estelle Larson's tongue. She almost spat them out, then stared down at the porch as if she could step on them.

"I never knew the deceased. I've been called in as an expert."

"Are you a pimp?" she asked primly. "That's the only kind of expert who'd have *any*thing to do with the likes of her."

"You didn't like her, did you?"

"She was my husband's client. And I suspect she was the cause of his death." Estelle Larson closed the door even more, as if shutting a portion of her past off from my view.

"How long had he been having an affair with her?" I thought this might get my nose broken, or at least the door firmly closed in my face. Again the woman surprised me.

"Five years. That's probably how he got the account." Her eyebrows rose slightly. "Have I shocked you, Mr. Thorne? Of course I knew about it. There's not much Benjamin does—did—that is a mystery. He's a very transparent man."

"How long have you been married?"

"Too long," she snapped. Estelle Larson heaved a deep sigh. "I never liked Ms. Santorini. I can't even say I am sorry she's dead. I'm not even sure if I am sorry Benjamin is gone."

"Your husband made a great deal of money off Priscilla Santorini's investments, didn't he?"

"I suppose. He was very good at what he did. Getting him to do it is another matter. You must excuse me, Mr. Thorne. This isn't the best of times for me."

"One final question, Mrs. Larson."

She fixed clear gray eyes on me. Her thin lips pulled back slightly into what must have been a smile. "I know what you're going to ask. The answer is no, I did not kill the slut." She closed the door and left me standing on the porch.

I heaved a deep sigh. Estelle Larson hadn't been what I expected. But I did believe her. She hadn't killed Priscilla Santorini—but I wouldn't be a bit surprised if she had killed her husband. I tried to place her as the woman in the elevator but couldn't. Not really.

And it didn't matter. Both the quartz knife and the *shuriken* in Benjamin Larson's neck has been wielded by a man.

The walk back to my apartment left me cold, tired and even more at odds than before.

CHAPTER SIXTEEN

The oyster bar served the best bagels this side of New York. I worked on a cinnamon-raisin bagel while I waited for Barbara Chan. The trade in fresh oysters was brisk. I watched people eating the slimy, tasteless things as if they were good.

"Order me a dozen?" came Barbara's voice. I looked over my shoulder. She stood behind me, smiling. "And another dozen for you?"

"I don't like oysters," I told her. "It's like eating snot."

"Oh, yuck," she said, making a face. "I guess the oysters don't have much taste. It's the sauce you dip them in."

I caught the waiter's eye and indicated Barbara's desire for the foul hunks of slime. "If you like them for the sauce," I said, "just order that and skip swallowing the oysters. They're alive, you know."

Barbara blinked. "I had never thought about it. They *are* alive, aren't they?"

"Eating dead ones would kill you in short order. But let's not talk about that." I paused for a moment, then said, "I'm sorry I upset you the other day."

"I'm the one who ought to apologize for running off like that. You touched old memories. It scared me that they were still painful."

"Your parents?"

"Both of them died from cancer," Barbara said. She sucked in a deep breath. I liked the sight, and she saw that I did. She smiled wickedly. "Are you sure you don't want any oysters? No? I see you don't need them."

Her hand drifted under the table and lightly brushed across my crotch. I wondered if she was an exhibitionist and would get off on making love in some semipublic place. Probably.

She pulled back to let the waiter deposit the plate with its shaved ice and oysters on the half shell in front of her. Then she dived in with a gusto I could only wonder at.

"It's just as well," I said, "that you weren't with me when I called on Benjamin Larson."

"I heard about it." She shivered. "Have the police uncovered anything more? Have you?"

"There's not much new," I admitted. "This isn't the kind of case where new evidence will instantly reveal the murderer," I said, thinking out loud. "The evidence is already in front of us." I went on to tell her that I was reasonably sure that the same person had killed both Santorini and Larson.

"You're still sure a man killed them?"

"The impression is too strong to deny," I said. "The knife's vibrations are overwhelming. The hatred—the *masculine* hatred of women—swamps all detail. The murderer is a man."

I went on to tell her about Estelle Larson. I concluded, saying, "She's the kind to kill her husband, not the other woman. But I don't think she did kill him."

"It sounds as if she'd come to some acceptance of her husband's affair with Santorini. That might come from knowing a large hunk of their income came from her account.

"Hackett's a drug dealer and Damien Bishop is just slime," Barbara said. She swallowed the last of the oysters and licked her lips. She smiled wickedly and said, "It's true."

"What is?"

"Oysters do make you horny." Our eyes locked. I reached across the table and took her hand and squeezed.

"The oysters have nothing to do with it. You're always this way," I said.

"True. But the oysters were good."

Her expression changed just enough to put me on my guard. I liked the former. The latter bothered me.

"What's wrong?" I asked her.

"I've been trying to duplicate the experience we had . . . that morning." Barbara shuddered at the memory of the small sojourn we'd taken when Priscilla Santorini had died. The screams from the quartz knife must linger in her mind, too.

"It's not been easy," she said. "I really don't know what happened when we were . . . together."

"Was it hypnosis? Did I cloud your mind? Want to see my fire girasol ring?"

"Peter, please. This is no joking matter. I think it's important I get some understanding of the experience so I can better design my experiment."

"Are you sure you want to continue?"

"No. No, I'm not sure. I mean, oh, never mind." Barbara stared down at the table for a few seconds, then blurted out, "I'm trying to find out more about the shovel."

The black cloud, the crushing weight, the experiment she had run in the ER. I shivered, but the crystal blade had replaced much of the dread I had endured from the shovel. There was more than enough in the world to keep me awake at nights with my heart pounding and my body bathed in sweat.

"It's not important, Barbara."

"But it is, Peter. If I can show Dr. Michaelson you sensed something we had no idea about, it'll convince him."

Her naivete in this matter was almost touching. Michaelson wasn't going to be convinced, no matter what facts surrounding the shovel Barbara dug up. The pun made me smile. She thought it was just for her.

"I'm going to keep working on the Santorini matter. The New Age aspects intrigue me, but the knife—" I had no words to describe the horror and dread that blade generated in me.

"Who else was on Cunningham's list?"

"Two more names, both women," I said. "I'm sure a man killed Santorini, but one of them might be able to cast some light on what is becoming an increasingly obscured crime."

"May I come along? I don't have to be back at the lab until late this afternoon."

"I'd enjoy your company. I didn't drive. We'll have to make do with either public transportation or walking."

"I'm used to it. My car is always in the shop," she said. "And I enjoy being with you." Her bold gaze didn't require a telepath to interpret.

"And I enjoy your company, as well." I didn't get a chance to say any more. She slipped under the table. Where her hand had fluttered a few minutes earlier, I felt hot breath.

"Barbara—" I gasped and tried not to show any reaction. She was an exhibitionist—and this wasn't a semi-public place. Anyone passing by the table could see what she was eating. I closed my eyes and tried to enjoy the sensations. I ended up enduring. This wasn't my idea of fun. I'm a more private person.

Barbara slipped back from under the table when she finished. She grinned broadly and licked her lips. "Where do we go from here? Who's left on the lieutenant's hit parade?"

Considering what had happened to Larson, I wasn't sure she was entirely wrong, even if she'd meant the remark flippantly. "Rhonda Poulan and Andrea Schulman. I don't know either of them, but Rhonda Poulan's husband is richer than Croesus. She and Santorini travelled in the same social circle. Philanthropy, the opera, that sort of public exposure."

"Royce Poulan," Barbara said. "I've heard of him. He owns a shipping company. A cruise line, with the fancy vacation ships like the Love Boat."

I nodded. Santorini's friends spanned the social spectrum, from drug dealers like Hackett to brokers to the wives of fabulously wealthy men. I was forming more of an opinion of them than I was of the deceased—and that was a major lack. Knowing who Santorini had been might be the piece of the puzzle that let me see who had killed her. All I knew about her was her dabbling in New Age mysticism—and witchcraft and drugs and anything else that might furnish a moment's diversion.

That she was having an affair with Benjamin Larson was obvious from his reaction to my questions and the brief psychometry I'd done on his desk set. Beyond the drugs, what she and Steve Hackett had going was less clear. Hackett was still in the sweepstakes for most likely to kill, as was Damien Bishop. The fiery-tempered astrologer would be the perfect murderer, in my opinion. I just wished I had gotten some sense of his guilt through psychometry. There had been only the flash of military might, not murder in his office.

"The Poulans live back in the area around the Larsons," I said. "Let's take a taxi. It's faster."

"And we can sightsee along the way," Barbara said, being a tourist far from either of our intentions.

The ride went by too quickly. The cab driver was probably sorry to see the fare end so soon. He had moved his rearview mirror around to watch us, probably the only thrill he got out of his job. I don't think we disappointed him too much.

"What a snazzy place," exclaimed Barbara. "One day I'd love to have a house like this."

I had to agree. The Larsons lived well. The Poulans' mansion put the other to shame in size, in design and in execution. The grounds were as well kept as the Arboretum or the Japanese Gardens in Golden Gate Park.

"Do they trim the lawn with cuticle scissors?" Barbara bent over and ran her hand along the close-cropped grass. "Maybe it's that genetically bred stuff that doesn't grow fast." She looked up at the house and marvelled at how well it was integrated into the lawn and slight rise. "Yes, this is the kind of place I want."

"Physicists don't make the kind of money it takes to keep up the grounds, much less the house," I said. "For that matter, I'm a magician and I couldn't conjure enough money." We went up the tightly winding path and I realized the appearance was deceptive. The grounds weren't as spacious as they looked. The clever landscaping produced the impression of vastness. Like so many lots in San Francisco, this wasn't all that large.

"What are we going to say to her, if she's even here?" asked Barbara.

"We wing it." I had no better idea how to approach Rhonda Poulan than I had Estelle Larson. At least, I didn't have to dance around asking really hard questions since Rhonda Poulan's husband hadn't been murdered the day before.

The sweeping veranda circled the house and gave a magnificent view of the city and the Bay. From the far side I was certain the Golden Gate Bridge would be visible. I'd barely stopped at the front door when it opened. A flustered-looking woman stared at us.

"Are you here already? Good, I mean, I don't want to rush you. I'm glad you're here early, but I wasn't ready for you."

"Mrs. Poulan?"

"Of course I am. Who else do you think called you?" She looked past us to the driveway and didn't see any vehicle. She frowned, as if working over a difficult problem. "Where's your truck? Don't all plumbers have trucks?"

"Mrs. Poulan, we're not plumbers," said Barbara. "We'd like to speak to you about Priscilla Santorini."

More confusion spread over the woman's plain face. Her hand fluttered to her throat. The expression changed as Barbara's words filtered into the woman's brain. I worried that she might be having a heart attack. The pain was transitory and the confusion returned—or was it merely a mask Rhonda Poulan showed to the outer world? I couldn't tell.

"Priscilla? She's dead. But she will be back."

"What?" Barbara stared at her in amazement. "I'm sorry, did you say she'd be back?"

"Oh, yes, she'll return. She'll be reborn. That's what we both believe. I've lived many lives before this one, many much more interesting."

"Dealing with plumbers is never fun," I said, knowing more about her now than before. Many of those dabbling in New Age mysticism believe in reincarnation, the migration of their soul from one generation to the next. Most of these people lead lives of quiet desperation and seek excitement through channelling. To have been a pharaoh or a French courtesan or an invincible conqueror appeals more than their humdrum everyday real existences. And for others, the knowledge that their spirits will move on into better quarters after their deaths is a comfort.

"You're so right. But what does my stopped-up drain have to do with Priscilla?"

"Mrs. Poulan, may we come in?" asked Barbara. She shivered lightly, giving silent reason for the woman to extend some hospitality. The wind had died down, but Barbara had found the right excuse.

"How impolite of me. Of course, do come in, please, this way, this way." Rhonda Poulan gestured toward the dark insides of the house. No lights were on and the sun had been under a heavy rain cloud most of the day. I blundered through the almost impenetrable murk until we emerged into a sitting room. The decor fit the mansion. Every piece of the rich, highly polished furniture was impeccably placed for effect. The room had a cozy look to it. Unlike many places where sitting on five-thousand-dollar antiques made me uncomfortable, the furniture looked used and usable.

"You shouldn't worry about Priscilla," she said. "I know it was a terrible thing, but she will be back. We channelled many times and meditated under a copper grid to bring our auras into alignment." She sighed, then added, "Her past lives were full and exhilarating. I'm certain her new one will be, too."

"Mrs. Poulan," I said before Barbara could inquire about channelling and the other things she had mentioned, "do you have any idea who might have wanted to kill Priscilla?"

"The world is filled with evil of all kinds. We can only try to perfect ourselves."

This simple answer was apparently all she needed to keep her content.

"Had you ever seen the crystal knife used to kill her?" asked Barbara.

"Oh, yes. She bought it some time back. I was never sure what she wanted it for. It had nothing to do with balancing energy flow." Rhonda Poulan looked around and said in a conspiratorial whisper, "I always wear green to bring myself into congruence with the growing things." She fished around inside the scoop neck of her elegant silk blouse and pulled out a large crystal pendant. "This focuses my healing energies. It's amethyst."

"What does your husband think of your New Age beliefs?" I asked.

The woman became a classic example of body language. She folded into herself, arms and legs crossing. The pendant vanished and her expression bordered on fear.

"He doesn't believe."

"That's a pity," I said carefully. I didn't believe in much of the New Age doctrine, either, except for the need to work toward personal growth. Sitting under a copper screen or paying thousands of dollars for rebirthing to learn how to cope with birth trauma struck me as both bunk and bunco.

"You're not going to tell him, are you?"

"Tell him what?" asked Barbara in all honesty.

"Oh, thank you. It's so hard being here alone most of the day."

"You don't have any servants?" I asked.

"My husband sees no reason to maintain a permanent staff. We contract out whatever needs doing." She smiled almost shyly. "And I do so enjoy cooking. I enjoy it almost as much as I enjoyed being with Priscilla."

We'd come full circle to Priscilla Santorini. "She was a special person," I said.

"She was. Her life was ever so exciting. The people she knew! She'd been everywhere and done everything."

"She certainly had a full circle of men friends," said Barbara. "How did she balance so many boyfriends? I could never do it. That must have been a juggling act to keep them apart."

"You know how she was," said Rhonda Poulan. "Never the same man twice in any week." The way she said it made me think she might have been privy to more of the deceased's secrets than she'd revealed.

"Too bad about . . . him," I said. "What he did to her."

"Who?" Rhonda Poulan looked confused again. I'd hoped to draw her out but had only flustered her.

"You know who I mean. The man she was seeing just before her . . . death."

"I don't think she was seeing anyone special. Though she might have been seeing—well, I can't mention *that*."

"What's that?" Barbara said softly.

"It's a secret. She told me to never, ever tell anyone. I can understand why, too."

"Why's that?" I asked.

"Why, it's not the kind of thing you discuss in polite company. Priscilla was right in not wanting me to talk about it."

"Does it have any bearing on her death?" I wondered if there was any real secret or just something Santorini had told this poor sensation-starved woman.

"I never thought on it. It just might." She frowned, then shook her head. "No, it couldn't. It's not *that* kind of secret. But it is awful, nonetheless."

I motioned to Barbara to keep Mrs. Poulan talking while I wandered around the room. I took a deep breath and began touching objects at random. Rhonda Poulan glanced at me and frowned in disapproval. She didn't like anyone touching her keepsakes. I understood that but needed some psychic input to work on.

Fear rattled through me when I touched a picture of her and a man I took to be her husband. It wasn't just fear. It was *fear*.

"That's my husband, Mr. Thorne," she said. "It was taken on our fifteenth anniversary. We went to Paris. It was so romantic."

Her words did not match with her tone. What should have been a cheerful, even joyous memory was laced with doubt—and again, *fear*. Rhonda Poulan worried about her husband's fidelity. She worried about her health. She worried about worrying until she was riddled with doubt. No wonder she seemed perpetually confused. She lived in a world where everything was suspect and dangerous to her personally.

"He wouldn't stray, Mrs. Poulan," I said distantly. "He isn't like that."

"I beg your pardon?"

"Nothing." I yanked my hand from the picture frame, noticing I'd left greasy fingerprints on the golden edge. I did what I could to remedy the intrusion. "Do you have any pictures of you and Priscilla?"

"No," she said, slipping into her conspiratorial whisper again. "Priscilla never liked having her picture taken."

"How odd for someone in the public eye so much of the time," said Barbara. "But tell me more about channelling. It sounds fascinating."

Barbara had found the doorway into the woman's soul. Rhonda Poulan began speaking earnestly about her ascension chamber in the basement and how she had harmonized and balanced it with Damien Bishop's help.

"I had a prediction done by Damien," I said. "It was a remarkable work." Actually, Bishop had called me a son of a bitch and had said he would see me in hell, but it was a prediction of sorts.

Again, the woman curled into herself. I had touched on something she didn't want to discuss.

"You know Damien personally?" I pressed.

"Of course. He did the horoscope for Andrea Schulman." Getting this from her was like drawing blood. I started to touch another of her belongings but stopped when I saw the surge of fear turning her pale.

"Are you afraid of Andrea, Mrs. Poulan? Was there something Bishop's horoscope warned you about?" My psychometry was giving me a "background noise" of undifferentiated fear. She lived trapped in a wide array of her own phobias.

"He did it for Andrea, not for me. I can't talk about it."

"That's the secret Priscilla told you about?" Barbara was incredulous. I didn't blame her. This was hardly anything to keep under wraps. People had horoscopes done all the time and, like palm reading or phrenology or tarot, they gave only general hints. Filling in the details was left to the recipient's imagination.

The only reason I pursued the point was that Andrea Schulman was the final name on the list of the dead woman's intimates. Mrs. Poulan was afraid of Schulman, but then she was afraid of everything from dust bunnies to her husband leaving her for another woman.

The doorbell rang. Rhonda Poulan shot to her feet and rushed off, fussing about the plumbing. I heard the rattle of tools and saw a burly man carrying a toolbox pass in the hall. Mrs. Poulan glanced toward us, unsure if she should ask us to leave. She followed the plumber into the kitchen.

"I don't think we're going to get anything more from her," said Barbara.

"Anything more?" I said sarcastically. "All I've seen in her is fear. She's frightened of her own shadow."

"And Andrea Schulman's, too," said Barbara.

I shrugged. It seemed that way.

We made our way out, unsure if we'd learned anything of importance other than that people who live in fine houses aren't necessarily happy being there. Rhonda Poulan would rather be wandering the misty corridors of her mind, inventing better, less fearful former lives for herself.

CHAPTER SEVENTEEN

I glanced at my watch. I'd made an appointment to see Andrea Schulman. I was already ten minutes late and would be thirty by the time I got to her office on Market Street.

"I wish I could go with you," said Barbara. "I really helped when you were talking to Rhonda Poulan."

I gave her a quick kiss, which she didn't want any part of. She made it much deeper, much, much deeper. It was with some reluctance that I broke it off.

"You've got to keep Michaelson happy. Show up for your meeting. He's expecting you."

"You're no fun, always talking about duty and that crap." Her words were chiding, but I knew she felt strongly about her schooling. She might believe the afternoon meetings with her advisor were fruitless, but she would always show up, if she could. Barbara Chan wasn't the kind to lightly pass on her responsibilities.

"I'll let you know how it goes," I said. "But I'll miss her completely if I don't get a move on."

"Okay." For a moment, Barbara looked frightened. She reached out and took my arm. "Be careful, Peter. I don't want anything to happen to you."

"It won't." I almost asked if she'd gotten some premonition, but stopped. She had shown no evidence of psychometric ability on her own—or any other paranormal talent.

I didn't have time to take a bus, and the cable car line was a ten-minute walk away. I strode the ten blocks to where I had my BMW garaged and jumped in. Zipping in and out of traffic and luckily finding a parking lot with an open slot just south of Market let me reach the office of Pacific Rim Enterprises forty minutes after our appointment.

The receptionist looked up when I walked in. She was dressed more like a high-fashion model than a receptionist. Her red hair was perfectly coifed, and the intricately decorated long fingernails showed that she did little more than answer the phone. Someone else worked as secretary, with its nail-damaging potential on a keyboard. I flashed her my best smile and said, "I'm here to see Ms. Schulman."

A flicker of disgust crossed her face. I knew I'd missed my chance.

"Ms. Schulman is in conference for the rest of the day. I'm sorry. When you didn't come, she had to—"

"It's entirely my fault," I said, and it was. "If traffic hadn't delayed me, I could have come closer to being on time. Is there a time when we can reschedule?"

"I don't know. This is a very busy time for us. All our executives are meeting with the Japanese trade ministers."

"MITI?"

"Why, yes," the red-haired receptionist said, looking for the first time as if I might be human. "Does your business with Ms. Schulman have to do with the meeting?"

"No, it's about . . . something else," I said. "I do need to speak with her before next week, if possible."

"It might be," the woman said. "Ms. Schulman left a note for you." She fumbled in a file folder at the side of her wide desk and passed the memo to he.

I took it, concentrating for a moment more on the psychometric feelings than the words neatly printed on the sheet. Andrea Schulman hadn't held the paper long enough to leave a portion of herself on it. Faint glimpses of a busy woman came to me and that was all. For all I knew, the receptionist had handled the note more than Schulman. I glanced at the message.

"Is there a time she mentioned for rescheduling?" asked the receptionist.

"No, she just gives her regrets."

"Do you wish to leave a message for her?"

I thought for a moment. My amateur nosing around had yielded little, and I had to prepare for my coming show. Getting a new assistant was the easy part. Ross had recommended a woman who had been working at L.A.'s Magic Castle with a mutual friend. Breaking her into my act would be the work of a single afternoon. But the rest! I had to practice.

I was willing to let Cunningham deal with Priscilla Santorini's murder, and Willie Worthington could track down Steve Hackett and pin drug and murder charges on him better than I ever could. I should have just said no and walked out.

"Tell Ms. Schulman this concerns a mutual friend, Priscilla Santorini."

The receptionist looked up sharply and started to say something. She clamped her mouth shut abruptly and bobbed her head. A single strand of red hair dipped across her forehead. She didn't notice.

The slight imperfection made her seem a little more human. But only a little. I smiled and left. I had the feeling Andrea Schulman would be getting back to me soon enough.

CHAPTER EIGHTEEN

I stretched, working to ease my stiff joints. Barbara had fallen asleep on my arm. When I moved, it disturbed her. She moaned and rolled over in bed. One large dark eye opened and stared at me.

"Sorry," I said. "I didn't mean to wake you. The circulation is starting to leave my arm."

"I thought we'd gotten your circulation speeded up. Should we go back out on the balcony? Maybe we should lean farther over the edge this time. It's only twenty stories to the ground, after all." She rolled against me, her tongue moving in a quick, darting motion.

"Don't do that," I said.

"You don't like it? You did before."

"Too much salt is bad for you," I said. I rubbed at the trails of sweat and sat up in bed. Seeing her every morning wouldn't be bad, I decided. Even with her hair mussed and her eyes still heavy from sleep, she was gorgeous.

"When are you going to get ready for your gig?" she asked. "I've never seen a magic act before." She grinned, then added, "You did do a good job of making this disappear last night."

She grabbed me and I wiggled away.

"Really, I've never see a magician working on stage. What's it like?"

I grinned as I remembered what it was like. There was a curious oneness with the crowd and, at the same time, a detachment as I concentrated on the tricks. The applause was nice, but their rapt attention during the act was better. I controlled them with my skills.

"It must be like a rock star or any other performer. You're center stage, people are watching and it's the finest feeling in the world."

"The finest?" she teased, grabbing me again.

"The second finest," I allowed but wasn't sure if I was lying.

"Are you going to keep on looking into the Santorini death?"

"I might," I said. "There are aspects of it that make me feel the same way as performing. I enjoy the notion I might be tracking down a killer, yet I'm repelled by the knife. The sound isn't like anything I'd every heard. And Larson's death is tied in. I can't put the pieces together. Did the woman I bumped into in the elevator have anything to do with his death?"

"I heard the knife scream, too," she reminded me. "It was awful, but I've heard worse."

"When you get more experience with entering the trance state, it might be more intense for you. For me, it's as if someone rubbed sandpaper across my soul."

"Is that why you want to keep on? You've never heard anything like it before?"

"I can't imagine what imprinted the knife—*who* gave it such a powerful message of pain and anger."

"Does it have to be someone on Lieutenant Cunningham's list? Why couldn't it be an aborted robbery attempt? The robber might have startled her, killed her, then panicked and ran."

"The knife," I said. "The killer knew her. The killer knew her and hated her."

"So it's got to be Steve Hackett or Damien Bishop?"

I nodded. It seemed logical that, if a man had committed the brutal crime, it was one of them. They were the only men involved with Priscilla Santorini at the moment who weren't dead. A drug dealer and an astrologer. Which was it?

As far as I could tell from my psychometry and gut instincts, neither had done it.

"I'll talk to Mrs. Poulan or Estelle Larson again. Neither of them killed Santorini, but they might know more than they've told me."

"And you missed Andrea Schulman. She must figure in somehow. Remember what Rhonda Poulan hinted about her."

"Bishop had done a horoscope. Big deal," I said.

"That's all nonsense. The stars don't reveal anything about our lives, past or future. Damien Bishop lives off gullible people willing to pay for a comforting word here and there mixed in with dire warnings."

"Let's not talk about him," she said. "Tell me about channelling. It sounds interesting. I wanted to ask Mrs. Poulan more, but the plumber came."

"There's not much to it. The New Age techniques involve a lot of rigmarole that's not needed. I don't believe that going into a trance can reveal past lives."

"But you can see the aura around inanimate objects and learn about whoever's held them. Why shouldn't you be able to see back into former lives?"

I sighed. The charge or field or energy that went into the aura came from a living creature. The stronger the creature, the more intense the aura. Most people leave their distinctive "prints" on keys and rings if they carry them long enough. Some forceful personalities imprint everything they touch.

The knife. The knife kept returning to haunt me.

"Let me put it to you on a more scientific basis. Humans generate energy to stay alive. We lose some through heat, through friction, through the action of our muscles and organs."

"Sure," Barbara said. "We replenish by eating."

So far so good. "Consider your DNA now. That's the determining factor of who you are. Does it seem reasonable that this is the basis for channelling or racial memory or whatever you want to call it?"

"I suppose," she said.

"Your DNA comes to you from both your father and mother."

"Half from each," she agreed.

"Go back a generation. Half of, say, your father's DNA came from his mother and father. That means you've only got one-fourth of your grandfather's DNA. And one-eighth of his father's, your great-grandfather. Go back ten generations. You've only got 1024th of that male's DNA. That's about two centuries. How do you focus in on such a small portion of your DNA? Why don't more recent 'lives' overwhelm the channelling?"

"Maybe we're selective or"—Barbara brightened as the argument came to her—"those personalities were the strongest and made the most imprint."

"Some channellers claim to go back millennia. The DNA from such ancestors must be measured in parts per trillion."

"The people who regress always claim they were pharaohs or conquerors."

"Some claim to read peasant lives," I countered. "There's some reason for being able to psychometrize. I see none for channelling, unless it's back a generation where the messages ought to be the strongest."

"I've never heard of anyone going back just one generation," mused Barbara.

"I doubt if you will. Inventing a life for your parents isn't as exciting as imagining you are descended from kings."

"It's easy enough to check up on your parents and their experiences, too. It's harder for someone who died in the Middle Ages," she said, getting the drift of my argument. "Are these people so bored with their lives? Like Rhonda Poulan?"

"That woman's afraid of everything. Santorini might have given her a doorway into a better world, even if it was just her own imagination."

"An overactive imagination might be the lady's problem, you know?"

I looked at Barbara and decided something else of mine was overactive at the moment. I showed her.

After we finished making love, I lay in a gauzy limbo, not sleeping but not awake. It wasn't the best time for making decisions, but I knew then I'd keep investigating Priscilla Santorini's murder. And Benjamin Larson's. There were too many unanswered and intriguing questions for me not to.

CHAPTER NINETEEN

"I don't see why it's necessary for you to follow me like this," I said. Barbara was getting on my nerves. Not only did the monitoring equipment I wore itch, it wasn't working up to her expectations.

"Just a few more adjustments. There's more interference than I'd anticipated. The gain isn't enough to send a clear signal. I'm getting jumbled readings. We don't want ambiguous data, do we?"

"No, we don't," I said as sarcastically as possible. The ridicule passed her completely. She was lost in a welter of LSI circuits and who knew what else. All I wanted to do was catch Andrea Schulman for a few minutes as she came home from work. What Rhonda Poulan had said about the dark horoscope kept elbowing its way into my thoughts.

"This won't take but a minute," Barbara said. It had already been ten minutes. I didn't want her hanging around my neck like the Mariner's albatross when I spoke with Schulman. Schulman was a busy woman, influential and probably unused to such nonsense as I was enduring. I didn't want to take up more of her time than I had to. It was already late afternoon, going into evening.

Leonard Cunningham had spoken to me earlier in the day and had told me to butt out of the investigation. I wondered who had protested my fumbling questions. Asking the lieutenant hadn't gotten me a direct answer. It sounded as if the complainer might have been Damien Bishop, but this was only guesswork. I had no good reason to poke around, but the crystal knife haunted me. Its shrieks rang in my ears. Worse, I was beginning to fantasize a hand gripping the quartz knife—and the knife tip was aimed for my heart.

That might have been nothing more than annoyance from wearing Barbara's electronics, though.

"There," she said with some satisfaction. "That will do it. I'm getting a cleaner signal now."

"Excuse me." I pushed past her and hurried into the lobby of Andrea Schulman's posh apartment house on Chestnut Street, not far from where Lombard Street leaves Hyde and wiggles its way down the hillside on its path across town to Coit Tower. The views were topnotch. I wondered if she was ever home enough to enjoy them.

"Ms. Schulman!" I called. Barbara had delayed me just long enough to miss her. The elevator doors slid shut and the cage began to rise. I slipped into the second elevator and punched the fifth-floor button.

"You're trailing wires," Barbara said, narrowly slipping past the doors as they closed. She began fiddling with two thin wires dangling from under my jacket.

"Hurry it up, will you?"

"You don't have to be this irritable. You agreed." Barbara scowled at me. Michaelson had given her a week to get definitive evidence of my abilities. Try as we might in the laboratory, nothing had registered on her equipment. This was the latest effort to make good. I wanted to help, but the paste holding the electrodes to my skin itched and I felt a compulsion to be at my top form when I talked with Andrea Schulman.

I started to tell Barbara to stop the experiment when the cage stopped and the doors opened. Andrea Schulman had put down an armload of packages and was fumbling for her key inside a huge purse. She was thrusting the key into the lock when I called out to her.

Startled, she spun. The keys fell to the floor and she stepped back, hand going to her throat. She let out a tiny squeak of relief when she didn't see any weapons.

"What's the meaning of this?" she demanded, getting back her poise.

"Here, allow me," I said. I stooped and retrieved her keys. I ran my finger along the notches and sides before she jerked them from my hand.

"Who are you to scare me like that?"

I introduced myself, then decided I had to tell her who Barbara was, too.

"A physicist? And a stage magician? You are the one

who missed an appointment with me yesterday.'' She sniffed and turned the key in the lock. "Whatever can a pair like you want from me?''

"Please,'' I said, helping her with the packages. "We didn't mean to alarm you. I just wanted a few words with you about Priscilla Santorini's death.''

"I've already told the California Highway Patrol everything I know—and it wasn't much. Priscilla and I were friends. We weren't good friends, just *friends.*''

"Casual friends,'' Barbara supplied.

"Exactly.''

Andrea Schulman was tall and well built. I suspected she might have been a body builder at one time from the way she moved and the way she filled out the expensive business suit with the red power tie. I didn't see any sag or bulge anywhere, and she was easily forty years old. She was a woman who kept in full trim, even if I was wrong about her possible hobby, if weight lifting can be considered such. Schulman kept her light brown hair short, almost butch, and must have spent a small fortune on the hint of wave in it. She was the epitome of a woman if not on top of her profession, then soon to arrive there.

"Where do you want this?'' I held the packages at arm's length. She vented a sigh of resignation, then motioned me into the apartment.

The interior startled me. It wasn't what I had expected from the woman. If I had been magically whirled away to the Orient, the room couldn't have been more intricately furnished. *Shoji* screens divided the main room from the dining area. A set of samurai swords stood on the mantel, the long *katana*, and the shorter *tachi* and *wakazashi* blades.

"You have some interest in Japanese weapons, Mr. Thorne?'' Andrea Schulman asked, a tinge of amusement in her voice. It wasn't merely amusement. She was laughing at me, feeling superior in her knowledge and my lack of it.

"Not really. I prefer the artwork you have so beautifully displayed,'' I said. Standing in front of one landscape showing peasants crossing a suspension bridge, I nodded knowingly.

"You like Hiroshige?" she asked. The voice came complete with its own sneer.

"I like most *ukiyo-e*," I said. "That one. The print of 'Red Fuji,' by Hokusai, is very nice, but rather common. I do admit to envy seeing you have a Harunobu." I indicated a print of two women in a small boat among the lily pads. "It dates from around 1760, doesn't it?"

"Yes," Schulman said in a low voice.

I swung around and looked at another, larger *ukiyo-e* print. "This one is 1775. Koryusai's 'A Windy Day.' Lovely. Such delicate lines and attention to flow. And the colors are superb."

"Are you an art critic?" she asked. "I know your reputation as a magician. I almost saw you once when you were performing at Radio City Music Hall."

"I'm flattered that you remember," I said, not bothering to hide the sarcasm. It was my day to be pestered by the insufferably superior. "I'm no art critic, though. I'm just interested in *ukiyo-e.*"

"How unusual."

I glanced from the woman to Barbara. She was busy working on the small receiver she carried. I had no idea what data she was collecting, but I'm certain she registered how irritated I was at Andrea Schulman's haughty attitude.

"Not many people appreciate Moronobu and the others I find so . . . stimulating," she said. She came out of her reverie over the beauty of the Japanese prints and glanced at her watch. "I'm very busy and my schedule is tight. What do you want?"

I looked past her to the dining area. She had removed the standard Western table and substituted a low Japanese one. Sitting on it was a delicately painted service designed for the *cha-no-ya* tea ceremony. She might be expecting important visitors.

"There are aspects of Priscilla Santorini's death that Lieutenant Cunningham wanted me to check out."

"A magician?" she scoffed. "How is this possible? Are the police so underpaid, overworked and lacking in intelligence that they recruit just anyone off the street?"

"It's not like that," Barbara said before I could answer. "He's an expert on New Age mysticism."

"And because Priscilla dabbled, *you* were asked to investigate?" She cleared her throat and made vague gestures with her hands. "Amazing."

"The crystal knife used to kill her was a product of New Age ritual," I said.

The woman's face hardened and a cloud of anger began to boil across it. "I know nothing about Priscilla's little games. I went to several parties at her house and we played out silly roles. Channelling, pretending to find ourselves in the past. That was a favorite of hers. Rebirthing. Pretending to remember the trauma as we were squirted from the womb. Bullshit. It was all bullshit."

"Then why did you participate?" I asked. From what she said, it was obvious she had been to the deceased's house more than once and engaged in the New Age rigmarole.

"We were friends. I'd met her somewhere else. Frankly, I don't even remember where or when exactly. It was several years ago in a different context. She had connections and promised me she would use them if I took part in her silly seances or whatever she called them."

"What sort of connections?"

Andrea Schulman looked disgusted. I wasn't sure if it was at herself for believing Santorini or at me for asking.

"Priscilla knew more importers than I did, and I'm in the business. I swear, she must have slept with everyone from here to the Orient and back."

"Are you saying she had—loose morals?"

"She was a whore, a slut. She'd sleep with anyone if she gained by it."

Again the public picture of the murder victim didn't mesh with the private. I had to believe she wasn't of the pickiest kind about who she had gone to bed with. Finding the murderer was looking more and more difficult. The killer might not be among Santorini's current circle of friends. A lover from years back might have turned up after nurturing a hatred for an impossibly long time.

"What did you hope to get from her?" I began wandering around the room, ostensibly enjoying the expert workmanship of her woodcuts. Beside the telephone an address book lay open. I glanced at it and saw several initials and phone numbers. They could have been anyone's. If Schulman was expecting someone soon, she might have just called a business associate. The secretary at her company had said she was chief negotiator for a lucrative contract with the Japanese Ministry of International Trade and Industry. Her interest in things Oriental seemed to qualify her admirably.

"Look," Schulman said in exasperation. "I knew her. I went to her house. It was lovely out in the woods, but I wouldn't have wanted to live there. She had hideous taste in decorating. Her beliefs bordered on the bizarre. All this New Age crap bored me. When she wasn't posturing and going on about how she had lived in previous times, Priscilla was an interesting person."

"And she had connections you wanted?" Barbara had asked the question I had wanted to. She was intruding, but I was glad Andrea Schulman turned her wrath on her rather than me. She was a fierce opponent.

"Hell, yes. Why else do people make friends? To use their connections. That's all there is. She knew people in Japan who could get me Tokugawa relics."

"The Edo Period?" I asked. "But those are all prohibited. The Japanese listed them as national art treasures after the war."

"Exactly, but anything can be had if you've got the money—and if you know the right people. Priscilla had both."

"And you had only the money," I finished for her.

Hot eyes burned into me. Her jaw set like a determined fighter's. The anger mounted dramatically, and I knew we had overstayed our feeble welcome.

"Thank you very much, Ms. Schulman. We must be going. Good evening."

She didn't quite slam the door after us, but I knew it wouldn't do much good to go back and ask if I could use her bathroom.

"An unpleasant woman," observed Barbara. "But it was interesting. I have full data on your responses during the time we were in her apartment. I can correlate these with your emotional state and get a much better baseline.''

"Wonderful," I said. Correlating my emotions was the last thing I needed.

"Don't be like that, Peter," Barbara said. "This is *my* life. I'm a physicist and we experiment."

"Sorry," I said. I was still disturbed and not sure why. It went beyond Andrea Schulman's rudeness. After all, I couldn't expect much more from her. I had badgered her for a meeting and had intruded when she had a visitor coming over soon.

"Call me if you find anything interesting." I bent over and gave Barbara a quick kiss. She nodded absently, playing with her dials just as she had played with mine the night before.

I got only a few feet when I heard her running after me. "To hell with analyzing the data," she said brightly. "I've put in enough time on this research."

We went to my place and continued her education and, to my surprise, mine.

CHAPTER TWENTY

Barbara hiked her feet up to the railing and leaned back, a drink sitting on the balcony beside her. A chill breeze blew off the Bay, but she didn't seem to notice. I did. I went inside for a sweater.

"Want to slip yourself into something warm?" she called.

"Later," I said, knowing what she meant. For the moment, I wanted nothing more than to stare at the ships slowly cruising along San Francisco Bay. I recognized a Canadian gun ship and a pair of U.S. missile frigates. Identifying them let me put my mind into a fugue state where nothing mattered. Sometimes my best ideas came this way, without forcing them.

"She was sure a strange one," Barbara went on when I sat beside her and took her hand in mine. "She was expecting company. I wonder who it was."

It was probably a business associate. She said she was caught up in the middle of negotiations with the Japanese trade delegation. My mind wandered. There was so much about Andrea Schulman that lay beneath the surface. I'd intended to ask her about Damien Bishop's horoscope of her and had not gotten to it. She had made me feel rushed.

And it hadn't helped that she had been so distant. Even the slightest hint of humanity would have helped me make some sort of contact and ask a few of the important questions. Rhonda Poulan was frightened of the woman. This I shrugged off. Rhonda Poulan seemed afraid of everything and everyone.

"There was a dead feeling to her apartment," I said, thinking aloud.

"What are you talking about? That place was a museum! The whole apartment was gorgeous. She had decorated it perfectly."

"She has good taste in artwork," I said. "The samurai swords were real, if I'm any judge." I had seen a few authentic *katana* and more than a few replicas. These had the feel of antiquity about them. Where Andrea Schulman had gotten art treasures like those, I couldn't begin to guess. Since the war, they had been on the Japanese proscribed list for export. Their government protected its past far better than we did ours.

"One day I'd like to be able to afford that kind of art," Barbara said. "But Chinese. A few nice T'ang Dynasty pieces, maybe."

"There was a nothingness to her place. Her keys had no imprint of her personality. The articles around the apartment were just as you said, like a museum. I got no feel about the real Andrea Schulman."

"No psychometry?" she asked. I felt Barbara shift into physicist mode. She hadn't told me what she had detected from the electronic gear I'd worn.

"You know I can't do it without some degree of concentration, but I do pick up random bits in casual contact. Her keys might have just been cut from blanks. If she had carried them very long, they'd reflect more of herself in them."

I thought hard. Schulman had expected someone. It might have been interesting to wait for a few minutes and see who her visitor was. I hadn't wanted to take the time, however. I was sorry about my distraction now.

"She's not your type, that's all, Peter," Barbara said. "She's all business. She saw right through you."

"Ms. Schulman doesn't seem to have much time for entertainers or even frivolous behavior," I agreed. "There wasn't a television in sight. And she doesn't strike me as the kind to have one in her bedroom."

"No, not at all," Barbara said in an almost dreamy voice. "She's a fine-looking woman, trim, lithe, moves like an athlete. Remarkable for someone in her forties, wouldn't you say?"

I didn't share Barbara's appreciation of the woman. Or maybe she was just baiting me, fishing for compliments. No matter how Andrea Schulman acted, no matter how astute her tastes in *ukiyo-e,* the art of the floating world, there was no hint that she existed. She had done what no one else in my memory ever had—she had lived in a distinctive apartment and imprinted nothing of herself on it.

"What are you thinking, Peter?"

"It's only been a couple of hours since we left. How long does a tea ceremony take?"

"Not that long. Just a few minutes." Barbara turned and looked at me. "You don't think her visitor is still there, do you?"

I shrugged. I doubted it. It would be a one-in-a-million chance. Pushing to my feet, I said, "I'll be back in a while."

"You're not going to leave me!" she protested. She joined me. "Andrea isn't getting any of your action while I'm around."

"Worried?"

"You were mighty interested in her . . . pictures," Barbara said. I couldn't tell if she was joking. It hardly mattered. Andrea Schulman wasn't my kind of woman.

Schulman's apartment wasn't far from mine. Barbara and I arrived in less than ten minutes. Now and then I think there is a special deity looking out for me. I found a parking place immediately.

"That's her apartment," Barbara said, craning her neck and peering up out of the car. "The lights are low. Romantic, you might say."

I considered possible courses of action. It was likely her visitor had come and gone. More than two hours had passed, but then I had no idea when her visitor was supposed to arrive—or even if there was one at all. It might have been a polite way of getting rid of me.

I smiled to myself. That didn't wash. If Andrea Schulman wanted me out, she wouldn't make up excuses. She wasn't that type.

After an hour, I grew impatient. Barbara convinced me to stay, if only for a bit longer.

"This is kinda sexy," she said, snuggling closer. "It's been years since I necked in a parked car."

"There, wait, Barbara, look!" I pointed toward Schulman's apartment. A dark figure slipped along the wall, just out of the bright glare of a security light in the entryway.

Even though I didn't get a good look at him, I knew who it was.

"Business acquaintance," I snorted. "So that's what she calls a business connection."

"Who is it?"

"Stay here," I ordered. "This won't take but a few minutes." I got out of the car and raced after my quarry. I turned the corner onto Hyde Street and almost bumped into Steve Hackett. He had his head down against the stiff wind blowing off the Bay and didn't see me. His expensive jacket was pulled tightly around his body. The way the wind pressed it into his torso, I saw I'd been conservative in guessing he had lost a considerable amount of weight. He was hardly more than a skeleton.

I took a few more steps, thinking to overtake him. Then I changed my mind. Nothing he'd say to me would amount to a hill of beans. He'd probably even deny he'd been in Andrea Schulman's apartment—and there wasn't any way I could prove him a liar.

Hackett had come to visit Schulman. I could only wonder why, but considering Worthington's interest in Steve Hackett, I knew it must have something to do with drugs.

With drugs and the Orient and maybe even *shuriken* buried in the throat of Benjamin Larson. But where did Priscilla Santorini fit into the picture?

CHAPTER TWENTY-ONE

The phone kept ringing until I lost my concentration. The trick I was practicing was simple but required considerable dexterity and timing. Giving in to the inevitable, I put the four coins and the playing card on the table and reached for the phone. I wished I'd remembered to turn on the answering machine. The beeps and annoyingly cute messages have become a part of everyone's life, but I hate playing telephone tag and don't use the machine unless it is necessary.

"Hello," I said, trying to keep the irritation from my voice.

"Whatsamatter, Peter, your dog just die? No, that can't be it since you hate dogs."

"Ever since the toy poodle peed all over the inside of my best silk hat," I said, recognizing Willie Worthington's voice and disgustingly cheerful tone. "You can't have found out what's in those hot dogs you eat or you wouldn't be this sunny and bright."

"I'm always bright, and Sonny is what my pappy always called me," he rattled on.

"I'm working—or trying to. Is this a social call? I've got to be on stage in a week."

"Legerdemain, eh?" he said. "Got to practice all the time, I bet."

"You'd win," I said. This time I didn't prime the pump. If he had something to say to me, he'd have to find a way on his own to do it. Almost guiltily, I looked at the coins and the card. Moving the four large coins along the top until one apparently fell through the card looks easy—and it is. All it requires are strong fingers and just a hint of showmanship. The fingers I have. The showmanship was what I had been working on when Worthington called.

"You still interested in Steve Hackett?"

"What? No, you've got it wrong," I said, interested. "You were the one who asked me to find out about him for you."

"We finally busted him on drug charges. He made a bad decision and tried to deal with an undercover narc." Worthington waited for me to respond now.

I had to practice my magic. My skills had become rusty in the month and a half I'd been away from the stage. This wasn't a big gig for me, but it filled the time and my bank account until a larger show opened for me. My agent had mentioned six weeks in Vegas. As much as I dislike that city, I love the cash flowing like an artesian spring there.

But my feelings about the Priscilla Santorini case were unresolved. I hadn't done anything more on it since seeing Hackett leave Andrea Schulman's apartment. I had thought long and hard about the ramifications of a Schulman-Hackett partnership and not much worthwhile had come out of it.

"Did you bust anyone with him?"

"Who did you have in mind? A user? Another dealer? His supplier?"

"Supplier, would be my guess," I said. Schulman certainly had contacts in the Orient. I didn't know how difficult it would be for her to smuggle in considerable amounts of heroin from the Golden Triangle in Laos.

"Hackett is playing it cool. He won't talk. You want to come by and have a word or two with him?"

"You want me to hold his hand?"

"Only if there's something to psychometry."

"You know I can't psychometrize living beings," I said.

"I hear hints of longing in your voice," Worthington said, baiting me. "You came across something about Hackett and haven't told me, right?"

"Do you think he knows anything about the Santorini murder? Or Larson's?" My mind raced. In spite of the pressure of time and my fumbling ways with simple tricks, the murders—and the damned crystal knife—still occupied much of my waking thought. How Hackett fit into the matrix was beyond me. He might have been the killer. Priscilla Santorini mixed her curious brand of New Age religion with drugs and sex. Hackett could have supplied both of the latter.

Finding out might be harder now. He could cop a plea to dealing and Lieutenant Cunningham would never see him in court—if he was the one who had killed Santorini. In its way, this was typical of the court system now. Get the felon off the street for as long as possible—or as often as possible. During the jail term, crime dropped and made everyone happier.

It would make Steve Hackett happiest of all if he did five years on a drug charge when he might otherwise have faced life in prison on a murder one charge. Or was it two charges of murder he was weaseling out of?

"Why don't you come on downtown and talk with him? There are enough guys lined up so's his lawyer will never be able to tell who belongs and who doesn't. Hell, I've got the DEA boys and girls jumping through hoops."

"Was he involved with the drug murders you wanted me to ask around about?"

"Come on down, Peter," he invited. "You ask the questions, you decide for yourself." Willie Worthington hung up, knowing I wasn't able to resist.

The pull of that damned knife was stronger than I'd thought, and all I had done was hear it as it sliced Priscilla Santorini's soul from her body.

I arrived at the ward room outside Worthington's office in less than forty minutes, record time for getting across San Francisco's rush hour traffic. Hackett sat in the gray-painted room, slumped over a metal table with more dents in it than the winner in a demolition derby. Something struck me as pathetic about the man, and it wasn't the notion that he was guilty as sin on the drug-dealing charges.

"Got company, Hackett. Wanna see Mr. Thorne?" Worthington moved to the side of the room so he could watch both of us and still let whoever stood behind the one-way mirror have a clear line of sight at Hackett.

"You're the geek who hit me up at Charade the other day," he said, staring at me with stone-dead eyes.

"And you're the one who went to Andrea Schulman's apartment four days ago," I said, watching his reaction closely. He only shrugged, as if it meant nothing. "Is she supplying you with heroin?"

"Heroin, me?" Hackett laughed harshly, then coughed. I thought his guts were going to come out into the hand he put over his mouth. "I don't touch that shit. No market for it since the mid-seventies. Coke, maybe crack, that's where the action is."

I went around the table and put my hand on his shoulder. He shied away like a nervous, apprehensive animal. I didn't disturb him more than I had to; I reached across the table and took the cigarette lighter laying there.

"What is this? You took my cigarettes. You taking my lighter, too?" The question went to Worthington. I ignored what the detective said. I slipped into a light trance as I held the lighter.

The flash that came turned my stomach.

Dead! Fucking dead!

I turned to the side and fell out of the chair, still clinging to the lighter. I heard Hackett say something about being drunk. Worthington didn't offer to help. I didn't want or need it. I lay on the floor and began curling into a fetal position.

Pain! Guts on fire. Burning, tearing, nothing left inside. The cold everywhere. Go away. Not me. No, no, NO!

"The darkness," I muttered, getting to my knees. I shoved the lighter across the table and pulled myself to my feet. "So big, so dark."

"What's this fucker talking about? You recruiting from the whackateria now?"

"I'm sorry," I said to Hackett. "How long do you have?"

"What are you talking about?" the drug dealer snapped. The deadness in his eyes flashed fear now.

"AIDS. You're dying of AIDS."

"Get him the fuck out of here!" Hackett screamed, leaping to his feet and overturning his chair. Two more policemen appeared like part of my magic act to restrain him. A third hung back, looking from me to Hackett and back.

It was this officer who asked, "Does he really have it? AIDS?"

I could only nod.

"Shit," Worthington said. "Get gloves on, dammit, before you handle him. And get him to a cell away from the others."

"Got a couple I'd love to put him in with," said one officer.

"You can't catch it from him," I said, finding my voice. "Not from just touching him."

"Sez you." The officer shoved Hackett ahead of him and out of the room. I sank into the one upright chair and shook.

"I don't think he's queer. He must have got it from a dirty needle. Who'd've thought an uptown dude like Hackett would use a dirty needle?"

"He might last a year," I said.

"Should test every last one of them we bring in here," Worthington grumbled. He took a deep breath and settled down, avoiding the chair Hackett had used. He parked his rump on the edge of the table and swung a leg back and forth nervously. "What else did you get from looking into his lighter?"

"He knows about the three dealers you're interested in," I said. "I didn't get many details. His denial of having AIDS overshadows almost everything. I don't think he killed them, but he knows who did."

"We can sweat him now," Worthington said. "Thanks, Peter." Worthington started to leave, then looked back at me. "Are you all right?"

"I'm fine," I said. "It's not every day I see into the life of a living dead man."

"You get used to it. I did."

I stared at Worthington and didn't recognize him anymore. "No one gets used to *that*," I said.

"You might be right," he said. His neutral tone spoke more than his words.

Sleep never came for me that night. The darkness all around crept too close.

CHAPTER TWENTY-TWO

"You look like homemade shit, if you don't mind my saying so," said Worthington. The detective rocked back in his creaking desk chair and hiked his feet to his desk. A hole had begun working its way through his argyle sock just above the ankle. He didn't seem to notice.

"You can't imagine what it's like moving inside someone's life," I said. The cup of black coffee I clutched sloshed back and forth. I didn't want it; I never drink coffee. The smell and taste make me sick to my stomach. I just needed something to hang on to and this was all Worthington had handy.

"Sometimes I really believe you can do all you claim," Worthington said, studying me like a bug under a microscope. I felt as if David Michaelson were in the same room. The atmosphere of disbelief was similar, yet Worthington had seen me psychometrize many times and even depended on my talent.

"What's the difference between doing what I do and making lucky guesses?" I put the coffee on the edge of his desk, obsessively lining up the bottom of the cup with an existing ring staining the top.

"I know how the guys who guess weights and ages do it. I don't have a clue about you, Peter. Are you sure you're all right?"

"I'm fine," I lied. The battered, mad interior of Steve Hackett's tormented soul had been laid bare when I went into the trance. The lighter had remained with him from the first doctor's appointment when he had been diagnosed as having an AIDS-related virus to the final visit almost six months ago when the doctor had verified Hackett's worst fears.

Every trauma had battered away just a little more at Hackett's brain and had given him the emotional power to imprint it all on the lighter. Outwardly, he still denied the truth of his affliction. How much longer he could do this was anyone's guess because deep inside he knew the fact of his illness.

Worthington looked up when another detective motioned to him from the door. He smiled crookedly and motioned the other officer away. "We got him," he said to me. "Hackett's confessing to just about anything we want him to."

"The murders?"

"He's spilling his guts. The DA is going to love us today. Tomorrow, who knows, but today we're going to be heroes." Worthington fumbled in his desk and pulled out his spiral notebook. He took the pencil from behind his ear and began writing in his meticulous, small handwriting. I had no idea what he was recording. When he finished writing, he spent a few seconds chewing on the pencil, then parked it behind his ear again.

"The way we figure it, Hackett knows he's got the auto wreck running around in his veins, so he's doing the most self-destructive thing he can by confessing." Worthington frowned. "He was a tough nut to crack. Real cool, you know?"

I barely listened to Worthington rattle on. I knew he was talking to give me time to put myself together. In its way, feeling the agony inside Hackett was as bad as listening to the crystal knife shriek with the resonance of Priscilla Santorini's death or sensing the utter cold-bloodedness of the *shuriken* taken from Benjamin Larson's throat. Holding out my hand, I saw that it had stopped shaking. I still felt lightheaded and remained seated.

"We might unravel half the coke trade in San Francisco, though I doubt it. I'm just happy to get the three murders off the books."

"What about Cunningham?"

"What's he gotta do with this? Oh, you mean you think Hackett will spill his guts about the Santorini thing?"

"He didn't do it."

Worthington stared at me. His mouth opened, then closed. The effect was similar to watching a beached fish gasping for breath.

My simple statement surprised me even more than it did Worthington, though I hid it better. Something inside Hackett had told me he was innocent of Priscilla Santorini's murder.

"He didn't kill Larson, either," I said.

"We can clear the slate of a lot of crimes," Worthington said. "Cunningham might want him for his case. The California Highway Patrol isn't prone to spend too much time investigating murders. They cover too much territory. Their work docket is loaded with twice the crimes SFPD's is."

"Hackett didn't kill her. And he didn't kill Larson."

"Hell, he didn't kill the three dealers, but he knows who did. That might make him an accessory—it makes him part of a coverup, if nothing else. We'll sweat him on the Larson case. If it ties in with Cunningham's case, we'll let him know. But we got Hackett first and the DA's not about to let him off the hook to go confess to every other murder one in the state."

"He doesn't know anything about Priscilla Santorini's murder," I repeated. Every time I said it, it became more of a fact to me. Hackett had nothing to do with the crystal knife or the *shuriken*.

"You're going to have to take that up with Cunningham."

It would be easy to pin the crimes on Steve Hackett. He was vulnerable, and he was guilty of other major felonies and he wanted to kill himself. Letting the law execute him was Hackett's easy way out. He might never have to face the truth of his illness.

But he had not killed Priscilla Santorini. Someone else had, and I knew I had to find out.

That damned knife refused to stay silent, even in my waking moments.

CHAPTER TWENTY-THREE

"There's nothing. Look. There isn't a thing on the strip recorder. Are you sure you . . ." Barbara's voice trailed off when she saw the stormy anger on my face.

"I went through hell," I snapped. "You can't begin to imagine what it's like to have AIDS and know you're going to die. Hackett accepts this deep down inside, even if he denies it outwardly. That's what makes it all the worse. He's looking for a way to kill himself so he'll never have to admit his disease to the world."

"You got all that from his lighter?" asked Barbara.

I nodded curtly.

"There's nothing on the readouts to show a change in your physiological responses," she said. She bent over the strip recorder and unfurled the graph paper like a war banner. "Until this point, that is. You show extreme agitation here."

"That was afterward," I said. "It took almost twenty minutes for me to get a grip on myself."

"That's about right," said Barbara, working on her charts. "Twenty minutes. Just about the duration Detective Worthington said he spent with you."

"There's nothing on your equipment? I'm wearing this rig for nothing?" I looked down at the tangle of wires under my shirt. Barbara had added even more sensors and had wheedled me into wearing them every waking hour. I wondered how far her receiver could pick up a transmission—or if I was carrying my own recording device.

"If I had to show this to a panel of other scientists, that's the conclusion they'd reach," Barbara said.

"To hell with this, then," I said, shedding my shirt. I began ripping off the electrodes. If they didn't measure anything more than the equipment she used in the laboratory, there wasn't any reason for me to wear the uncomfortable rig.

"I've got to talk with Dr. Michaelson tomorrow," Barbara said tiredly, "and there's not a shred of verification to back me up. I'm going to have to give up on this one for my thesis and go with one of his projects." She let out a deep sigh. "NMR work on rare earths isn't my idea of fun."

"This isn't mine, either. I just wanted to learn more about myself."

"It hasn't been a complete waste," she said, smiling. "You might not make the best research subject in the world for mental abilities, but you have other fun abilities."

"Thanks," I said dryly. I wasn't sure if that was an insult or not. Being wanted for only my body was a reverse chauvinism that didn't appeal to me.

"I didn't mean it *that* way. You know what I meant, Peter."

And I did.

"Since the experiment is a washout, let's have lunch. I'm hungry. How about you?"

"Not really, but I need the time to think. Maybe you can help me come up with suggestions to convince Dr. Michaelson about giving it one more try."

"Very well," I said. I put my shirt back on and rubbed at the spots where the saline paste still caked on my skin. Getting into the short street just outside the laboratory gave me the chance to breathe more easily. The lab held oppressive memories for me—not the least of those being the crushing black fog generated by holding the shovel. I put my arm around Barbara's shoulders and we started off toward Turk Street.

"We've come to a—" Barbara abruptly stopped and spun, glaring at a driver smoking down the street toward us.

A glint off the barrel of a rifle warned me. I dived for cover, my arm still around Barbara's shoulder and sending her spinning off balance. The rattle of automatic fire filled the street.

The only machine-guns I'd ever heard were in movies. The reality of the experience made the sounds surreal,

more than life and curiously nonthreatening. But I kept
wiggling and kicking in spite of the odd perception. Chips
of mortar and brick rained down on me from the impact
points against the building's wall. It didn't seem deadly,
but I knew any one of those slugs could snuff me out like
a candle in the wind.

"What's going on?" sputtered Barbara.

"Stay down!"

She tried to reach the door leading to the lab. The car's
tires smoked and screeched in protest as the driver wheeled
around in a narrow side street and came back. The
machine-gun clattered again. White-hot pain seared along
my side and sticky wetness exploded. My new shirt soaked
up some of the blood pouring down my torso; the rest ran
down into the waistband of my trousers.

The machine-gun kept firing forever—or so it seemed.
I lay sprawled on the sidewalk, a pool of blood expanding
under me. The would-be killer tried to put a few more
rounds into me, but the car's driver had other ideas. They
sped off, leaving a trail of chopped-up vegetation from the
machine-gun burst.

Better a few bougainvillaea than me.

"Barbara," I croaked out. "Are you hit?"

"What happened?" she asked in a shocked voice.
"They shot at us! They shot at us!"

"Are you hit?"

"No, I don't think so." She stood and felt herself, as
if she expected to find an arm or leg or lung missing. Then
she saw my condition and turned pasty white. "My God,
you're shot!"

"It's not too bad," I said. I struggled to prop myself
against the building. The wound hardly hurt now. I had
been injured far worse during my stage escapes. This was
messier than it was dangerous.

In the distance echoed police sirens. Less than a minute
later, the street filled with cruisers, their blue and red lights
painful in my eyes.

"What are you doing?" cried Barbara, seeing them
come pouring out of their patrol cars, pistols drawn.
"We're not the criminals!"

The police approached us, service revolvers leveled. I wasn't in much of a mood to protest.

"That's my job," I called out when they spun Barbara around and frisked her, as if she were the criminal rather than the victim. When they did it to me, I almost passed out.

"We got an ambulance coming to help you," one cop said. He still held his revolver tightly, though he didn't aim it at me. "What happened here?"

"The usual," I said. "Academic squabbling turned nasty. You know how it is with the ivory tower types."

I thought he was going to cuff me and take me to the station for booking.

"We got some of the casings, Sarge," an officer said, holding up a plastic Baggie filled with spent brass. "Looks like a MAC-12."

"Ingram Arms' finest," muttered the sergeant. He turned and looked over his shoulder at a bulging black whale of a car coming down the street. Willie Worthington heaved himself out and came over. Worthington's partner got out of the passenger side, hitched up his pants and then rubbed his hands as if going to work.

"Thought you boys might want a little company," he said, flashing his badge. "We heard it on the squawk box and decided to check it out."

"Not your game," the sergeant said. "Nobody bought it."

"It wasn't from lack of trying," I said, still propped against the wall. "Can you get them to patch me up?"

"No need getting your fancy suit any more messed up than it is." Worthington shook his head. "That's going to be one hell of a cleaning bill. Blood's hard to get out once it dries. Least, that's what I've heard."

"You've never been shot, have you?" I asked.

"Never have. Only fired my gun once, and that was almost ruled an accidental firing," Worthington said, crouching down. He stared at the two officers holding Barbara. "You guys having fun? Let her go." Seeing that they obeyed, he asked me what had happened.

I told him as succinctly as possible. Worthington took a few seconds off to let the paramedics patch me up. The wound was about as I'd thought. A single 9-mm slug had slid along my floating rib, leaving a shallow, if bloody, groove. Sucking in air hurt, but nothing major had been shot up or broken.

"I'll get his statement. You boys can go back to ticketing jaywalkers," Worthington said. He got a cold glare in response. The sergeant cleared the street. In five minutes, only the paramedics remained. In ten, only my blood on the sidewalk and the chipped building facade showed that anything untoward had taken place here. Another detective had arrived and escorted Barbara into the laboratory, leaving Worthington and me outside.

Worthington looked around, then heaved a deep sigh. "What a mess. Was it you they wanted or was it her?" He jerked his thumb in Barbara's direction.

"It might have been a random shooting," I said. I couldn't imagine why anyone so emphatically wanted me dead.

"Not random," said Worthington. "They came back. If it had been some doped-up kids out on a lark, they'd have kept on going. Using a MAC-12 doesn't sound like any accident to me."

"May I?" I held out my hand for the bag filled with the spent brass. Worthington tossed it over, then began prowling the street, making his meticulous notes about the tire treads and recording who knows what else in his spiral notebook. He occasionally gnawed on the yellow wood pencil; but mostly he studied the street and the marks left.

I held the bag in my hand, cupping its contents. The brass was warm, not from firing but from the sun. I clutched it tightly, settling my mind and striving for the trance needed for psychometry.

I yelped when the first of the impressions came to me. *Coldness. More Americans dead. No loss. Need to spray bullets in wider fan. Missed last time. Shamed me. Shame! No finger. Kill myself if miss again.*

I put the bag of cartridges on the sidewalk beside me and tried to work through the welter of images that had crowded into my skull. Getting the psychometric impressions is relatively easy. Dealing with them, sorting them out, making sense of them later, is hard.

"So?"

"He was missing a finger," I said, hardly knowing I was speaking. "There wasn't any hatred in him. Not really. He was just out on a job. And tattoos. His entire body is covered with tattoos."

"A pro?"

"Maybe," I said. "He worried more about technique than who he was aiming at. There was an incredible sense of guilt—no, not guilt, shame—over a past failure. He had let his boss down and didn't want to do it again. The killer actually considered killing himself if he failed this time." That puzzled me. It didn't jibe with the idea of contract killers working only for money and devil take anything else.

"You're way in over your head this time, Peter," Worthington said. "Was it the little finger that was missing?"

"Yes," I said, realizing it had been. "How did you know?"

"Don't get your hopes up that I know the hit man. It sounds as if a *yakuza* came after you."

"What's that?"

"The Japanese equivalent of the Mafia, which of course, as every newspaper reader knows, doesn't really exist."

"Why? Why would this *yakuza* want to gun either Barbara or me down?"

"Ah, old son, you're going to have to tell me that. They usually only have falling outs among their own members. It's damned rare for them to come after a civilian. Do you think Barbara might have overseas contacts?"

"Ask her. I don't know, but I doubt it. Her parents are long dead." Worthington helped me stand. The wound in my side had caked over again from the slow oozing, but it didn't give me as much pain as it had even a few minutes earlier.

"Let's go give it a try. Burnside isn't going to be able to handle Barbara. Hell, Burnside has trouble handling his own dick."

Burnside must be the other detective. We went into the lab. Barbara sat at the desk, still shaken and pale but working to compose herself. The graduate assistant looked distraught, and I didn't think it was because of what had happened outside.

"I think she knows more'n she's saying, Willie," Burnside called out. "I say, let's take her downtown and sweat her a bit. That'll loosen her tongue."

"Burnside." Worthington motioned with his finger to a spot on the far side of the lab. The two detectives argued for several minutes. Burnside left, glaring at both Worthington and Barbara.

After the detective left, Worthington said to Barbara, "He likes you. Really." In a more businesslike tone, he added, "Don't worry about him. He gets a bit frisky at times."

"He wanted to arrest me!" she flared. "I don't know what happened out there!"

"And I believe it," Worthington said. "Really I do."

While Worthington and Barbara continued to discuss their mutual pain in the ass named Burnside, I settled into a chair.

"He says it was a *yakuza* killer who tried to gun us down."

The uncomprehending expression on Barbara's face told me more than words ever could.

"We must have stumbled across something about Priscilla Santorini that sparked this," I said. "I haven't been doing anything else to warrant a Japanese mob hit. Have you?"

Again Barbara's expression gave the answer before her words. She was even more at a loss than I was.

"You think your nosing around in the Santorini case brought this about?" asked Worthington. He scowled and chewed hard on his pencil. "What connection did she have with the Japs?"

"I don't know, but she had some," I said, remembering that Andrea Schulman claimed a friendship with the woman simply because of her many overseas contacts. Another thought occurred to me. "Could this tie in with Steve Hackett?"

"He didn't finger any *yakuza* when he was spilling his guts," Worthington said, smirking at his own feeble pun. The detective felt compelled to explain the joke for Barbara's benefit. "If they screw up bad, the *yakuza* hit men often chop off their own little fingers as a tribute to their bosses. Peter did his little psychometry trick with the spent cartridges and came up with a missing finger on the gunman."

"That's the only clue in this case?" Barbara looked frightened. I didn't blame her. Having the Japanese mob after you is far worse than having them buy all downtown Honolulu.

"Actually, I've got tons of others," said Worthington. "It all ties in. The preliminary report was of two Japanese in a stolen car."

He hadn't mentioned this to me. I wasn't sure if I appreciated him holding back any information. Worthington had his own ways of working, as I did. We'd both arrived at the same conclusion with different data.

"I got to file a report. I want both of you down to my office first thing in the morning. You're not dead, but I'm taking a personal interest in the case. See you, Peter." Worthington nodded in Barbara's direction, then left.

"You're still bleeding, Peter," she said. "Let me get you to the hospital."

"I'm fine," I said. "You don't have *any* contact with anyone in Japan?"

"Not really. I request reprints from Tokyo now and then. The department secretary takes care of that. I may be of Chinese ancestry, but I don't speak it. I certainly don't speak Japanese."

"The *yakuza* is a crime family," I said, reciting what Worthington had told me. "Like the Mafia."

"Do you think Priscilla was mixed up with them?" asked Barbara. "Did we touch a raw nerve somewhere?"

"I can't imagine where. Worthington doesn't think Steve Hackett had anything to do with the *yakuza*. From all Hackett said, that's probably right. His connections were in South America, not in the Orient."

"Mafia," Barbara muttered to herself. "I remember something about Senate hearings a year or two ago."

"So?" The pain was coming back in dull, aching waves. I wanted to get to a doctor and have my ribs properly tended.

"Rhonda Poulan! That's it! Her husband, Royce, was questioned about his link with organized crime."

Barbara and I looked at each other. No wonder Rhonda Poulan was constantly afraid, if her husband was a gangster. That still left too many questions unanswered.

"Let's go ask her about it," Barbara said, as if reading my mind.

"After a visit to the doctor."

"We've got a good med school," she said. "And I've got a friend who can patch you up. She'd love to do it—damn her eyes."

Seeing Barbara's med student friend, I saw the reason for her concern. I didn't know doctors could be so lovely. But then, I didn't know physicists could be, either, until I met Barbara.

CHAPTER TWENTY-FOUR

Barbara Chan drove my BMW. Moving presented something of a trial for me, and she seemed to enjoy the prospect of being behind the wheel of a car that didn't fall apart every few blocks.

"It won't take long for me to change my clothes," I said, worrying about getting blood on the car seat.

"I'll come up," Barbara said. "Don't argue." She smirked. "It'll be fun helping you change."

Helping me might take longer than I wanted, but something else made me agree. I didn't want to leave her alone. The *yakuza* hit men had escaped, after all. And returning for us was better than sacrificing still another finger to their uncompromising boss.

It took less than twenty minutes for me to clean up and get new clothing. With some reluctance, I let Barbara toss the ones I'd worn into the trash. Mending the shirt was out of the question and the blood stains on the pants were beyond cleaning. I chased her out and finished cleaning myself. When I went into the living room, Barbara had fixed a cup of herbal tea.

"Let's go," I said. "I want to find out if there's any connection between what happened to us and Rhonda Poulan." It struck me as unlikely that Royce Poulan would contract killers to remove us after we'd spoken to his wife, but events went on around us that were beyond ken.

"I'll drive, if you don't mind," said Barbara. She smiled wickedly. "I love driving that Bimmer of yours. Taking the turns makes me feel like a race driver."

I muttered something about dying, but Barbara ignored me. I let her drive. By the time we'd reached the Poulan residence, I was ready to recant. Barbara was hell on wheels in the heavy afternoon traffic. Somehow, we managed to arrive without losing even a chip of paint. I vowed to drive us back.

"What's wrong?" she asked, seeing the police cars before I did. I craned my neck and saw a half dozen cruisers, an ambulance—and Willie Worthington's black bulgemobile. Cold winds blew up and down my spine.

"Maybe we weren't the only ones the *yakuza* were after," I said.

"But why would Royce Poulan have his own wife hit?" asked Barbara. "That doesn't make sense."

My mind turned away from the husband as the source of our woe. There must be other possibilities. There had to be.

"Get on out of here," a uniformed officer said, waving us on around the driveway and back to the street. He paused, then asked, "Didn't I see you two earlier? Yeah, over at the college. You almost got gunned down."

"We'd like to see Detective Worthington," I said.

"He might want to see you," the cop said. From that I knew someone had died, gunned down in the way we'd almost been killed.

"Was it Rhonda Poulan who died?" I asked.

"Park over there. The suits are all in the house."

"Suits?" asked Barbara.

"The detectives," I explained. I touched Barbara's shoulder. Asking more questions here wouldn't get us real answers.

We wheeled around and slid into a space near Worthington's car. It was only a matter of minutes before another uniformed officer showed us to where Worthington and Burnside worked with a forensics crew in the entryway to the house. Worthington glanced up. He wasn't happy to see us.

"What brings you here?" he asked. "Not enough excitement in your drab, meaningless lives?"

"Who was it?" A body had been covered with a plastic sheet. The formless lump could have been anyone.

"Rhonda Poulan. Someone used a MAC-12 on her. A lot. Turned her to bloody Swiss cheese." Worthington held up a plastic bag filled with spent brass. "Do these look familiar?"

I took it and stared at the cartridges. Going into a trance and fully psychometrizing would give me some hint about the killer. I handed the bag back.

"Well?" demanded Worthington. "Is it the same guy who tried to off you and Doc?" He looked from Barbara back to me, fixing me with his hard stare. Worthington wasn't a happy camper. Someone almost killing us was one thing. Having the wife of a prominent citizen, especially one with ties to organized crime, shot to pieces was another matter entirely.

"I . . . I'm not up to checking," I said. The images would stay with me for days. "Do you have any clues?"

"It's the same weapon," Worthington said. "The forensics guys looked at the casings under a magnifying glass and saw similar scratches from a banged-up ejector."

"What happened?" Barbara looked pale. I put my arm around her for support. She leaned against me, which wasn't too good an idea. I wasn't any too steady myself. Too much had transpired this afternoon.

"Looks like someone walked up to the door and rang the bell, she answered, then the gunman opened up on her at close range." Worthington silently indicated the blood spatters on the walls. It had been a messy, if quick, death.

"The husband," Barbara said too fast. She showed her nervousness. "Royce Poulan was brought before the Senate on racketeering charges last year."

"We know," Worthington said in disgust. "We do our homework. These days all it takes is a few taps on a computer keyboard. Did you also remember he was exonerated? His partners in a building scheme on the docks were in cahoots with the mob. He wasn't."

"I didn't hear that," Barbara said.

"They never print stuff like 'so-and-so was found innocent' in the papers," Worthington said. "There's no sales in that. Royce Poulan may cut corners in business and not make anyone's Mr. Nice Guy list, but he seems clean." He took a deep breath. "Even in this."

"There's a tie-in," I said. "We speak to Rhonda Poulan and she gets killed—and we almost do. What did she know?"

"More to the point, Peter, what do *we* know?" Barbara asked.

"Maybe nothing. They might think she told us something she didn't."

"Are you getting messed up in this, too, Doc? Shit. You're too cute to get killed." Worthington shook his head. "I'm going to talk with the deceased's husband." Worthington spoke with some distaste. For all his fine words about Royce Poulan being found not guilty—or at least having charges dropped—he didn't think too highly of the man.

"Can we listen in?" I asked.

"Irregular," Worthington said. "In this case, it's probably a rotten idea. Why don't you hang around out here for a few minutes? If it looks as if you can fill in any blanks, I'll call you in." Worthington gestured to Burnside, who scowled. The pair left us in the entryway with the body.

In spite of myself, I kept glancing at the covered corpse. Rhonda Poulan had not been a cheerful woman, and she had not been someone I'd have ever felt comfortable with as a friend, but I had known her and she was dead. What really worked at my guts was that she had been killed because we had talked to her.

"This might not have anything to do with the Santorini case," Barbara said. "She might have gotten shot—and the two of us shot at—because of something her husband did."

Worthington had hinted at it, yet I had learned to trust my first instincts. The killers had come for me first, then come over here and finished the job.

"Peter? You two want to come in here?" Worthington stood in the doorway leading to the sitting room where Barbara and I had spoken with Rhonda Poulan less than a week earlier. We entered and saw a bulky, balding man hunched in a chair. He looked up. Cold anger filled him and he tried to place the blame on us.

"We're sorry this happened, Mr. Poulan," I said, knowing this had to be Royce Poulan.

"The detective says you talked with Rhonda."

"The day the plumber was here," I said.

"Yeah, I remember that. All she'd tell me was how much he charged. Eighty goddamn dollars an hour." He fought to hold back tears. His sorrow turned from cold anger to fire. "Somebody's going to pay for this."

"We're working on it, Mr. Poulan," Worthington said forcefully. "Without your cooperation, we can't find the killer."

"You won't. Hell, look at the way it was done. Professionals."

"We've got some idea who did it," Worthington said. "A man in a stalled car down the street can identify the killers." Worthington glanced at me and continued. "One had his little finger chopped off. The guy remembered this as being odd. That and they were both Japanese."

"That damned mysticism of hers got her killed," Poulan said, more to himself than to us.

"Can you explain that?" Worthington chewed on his pencil, ready to take notes.

"It was the people she hung out with. Christ, I never saw such a bunch of fakes in my life. Channelling they call it. A rip-off is closer. Reliving birth trauma to improve your life. Sitting in copper boxes to meditate. Did you see Rhonda's meditation chamber in the basement?" He snorted and rocked back in the chair.

"It's a pyramid made out of copper. That focuses some cockamamie energy, that and the million crystals she has around. And witchcraft? She tried that, too."

"With Priscilla Santorini?" I asked.

The tension in Royce Poulan's body made me wonder if he wasn't going to snap at any instant.

"That bitch," he snarled. "If she wasn't dead, she'd be the first one I'd go after."

"Because of harmless dabbling in New Age philosophy?" I put the question in as neutral a tone as possible. I didn't want him flying off on a tangent.

"She and the bitch were having an affair. Can you believe it? Rhonda worried I'd find a younger woman and leave her. She worried constantly about this and that—and not once, not once in twenty-three years of marriage, have I cheated on her."

"Not once?" Worthington's eyebrows rose a fraction of an inch.

"No."

The sharpness in Poulan's answer made me believe him.

"She was strange, I'll grant you that. She had crazy ideas, but I loved her. But she goes off with that stinking bitch and I get . . ."

"Blackmailed," I guessed. The expression on his face told me the answer.

"Whoever it was had pictures. They called and asked for money. I gave it to them."

"And?" prompted Worthington. "You were hit on for more?"

"Not a cent more. They stayed bought. I got the pictures in the mail. The postmark was up in Redding."

"That was it? You never had another demand for money?" Worthington scribbled notes.

"No."

"Unusual," the officer said. "Blackmailers never stay bought."

"Who do you think it was?" I asked. "Priscilla Santorini? Her death could explain why there wasn't another demand."

"I thought it might have been, but I don't know. I never talked to her. And hell no, I didn't recognize the voice on the phone. It was muffled."

"Male or female?" asked Barbara.

"Male, and what is this? A College Bowl team? Are you people cops, too?"

"Interested parties," I said. The man's expression told me even more. His arms crossed and he sat back, the body language completing the picture of total noncooperation.

"Don't worry about them. They're experts I called in," said Worthington. Burnside guffawed. "This one's a physicist over at the university. Forensics. She's a specialist in all kinds of scientific stuff."

"And you?" Poulan pinned me with his icy-hot stare.

"Are those Mrs. Poulan's keys?" I asked, pointing to a ring on the table beside the chair.

"Yeah."

"Let him look at them. He's a . . . lock expert," Worthington finished lamely.

Royce Poulan tossed me the keys. I grabbed them and stared at them. All but one were worn. I ran my finger along the edge of the newly cut key and tried to psychometrize. Nothing came. It was too new to have absorbed any imprint.

"What's this one for?" I asked.

Poulan took the ring back and went through the ring one key at a time. I watched his lips move. Car. Garage. Back door. Front door. Cabinet. When he came to the new key he stopped and just stared at it. He dropped the ring back onto the table.

"That's a new key. I don't know what it's for."

"May I see your keys?"

The man fished them out of his pants pocket. I glanced at them; none matched the shiny new key on Rhonda Poulan's ring.

"Where's this getting you?" demanded Poulan. "Are you going to arrest the men who did that?" His eyes drifted toward the hall where his wife's body was being removed.

"We'll let you know, Mr. Poulan." Worthington flipped shut his notebook and left the room. Barbara and I followed. To my surprise, Barbara hurried to overtake the detective.

"What *is* being done?" she demanded.

Worthington let out a gusty sigh. "Doc, I'll be frank with you. There's real good reason to believe this was a *yakuza* hit."

"You've got a description. And Peter and I can—"

"You can't do jackshit, Doc," snapped Worthington. "We're not going to catch the scum who killed her—or who shot at you. And I'll tell you why," he said, cutting off Barbara's outraged protest. "This is a professional job. The two, the driver and the shooter, are probably out of the country by now. Maybe en route to Japan, maybe in Hawaii waiting to get to Japan. Hell, I can't say."

"They can't be all the way back to Japan—or even Hawaii," Barbara said angrily.

"They're probably beyond our reach, wherever they are," Worthington said tiredly, seeing argument wasn't the way to deal with her. "It's a fact of life. We don't have the resources to track them down if they're out of the country."

"You've got to do *some*thing."

"And we are. We'll go through the motions, we'll do our damnedest, and it's not going to be good enough. I'm sorry the woman got hit. I'm sorry you got mussed up. But that's about where this whole mess will end. Excuse me, I got people to talk to." Worthington pushed past her and spoke at length with Burnside.

From the other detective's expression, Worthington was laying down the law. Burnside would have dropped the matter entirely. Worthington wasn't like that. Barbara might not believe it, but Worthington had already set into motion all the legal equipment he could. Finding the killers would be difficult.

I put my arm around her shoulders and pulled her close, as much for my own comfort as hers. The expression on her face was one I'd seen before. She had a holy war to wage.

CHAPTER TWENTY-FIVE

Barbara insisted on coming with me. After the last visit to Damien Bishop, I knew this was probably a mistake. She could never be objective about the astrologer after hearing what had happened to my wife. For that matter, neither could I, but I held my contempt for the man in check.

"Mr. Bishop is out today," the secretary in the fancy outer office said.

"We'll wait," Barbara said, barging into Bishop's office. It didn't surprise either of us that the astrologer sat behind his desk, fingers resting on the keyboard of his computer.

"What is this?" Bishop demanded. "I don't want to talk with you. Either of you."

"Rhonda Poulan is dead," Barbara said, as if it meant something personal to her. In its way, I suppose it did. What still gnawed at her gut was her own brush with death.

"A shame," Bishop said. "Did her husband kill her?"

"She was gunned down at her front door," I said, not liking the belligerent way Barbara approached this. Bishop would refuse to speak if she got too truculent.

"I know nothing about this," the astrologer said. "However, I cast a horoscope for her that showed these to be dark days. I had not read the influence of Pluto properly if she is truly dead."

"You think we're lying about that?" Barbara demanded. I moved slightly, forcing her to veer off as she advanced on him. This took the edge off any attack and gave her a chance to remember we wanted information, not bloodshed.

"I have no idea what you're doing," said Bishop. "What I wish you would do, though, is leave. I am in the

middle of intricate calculations on an important horoscope.''

Glancing at the screen told me nothing. The work that
went into such mumbo-jumbo did not interest me.

"Is it for Andrea Schulman?" I had asked this on the
off chance he might respond. His reaction was more than
I could have hoped for. Bishop turned white and his hands
started shaking.

"Don't you dare touch anything on my desk!" he cried.
He threw himself over the papers scattered there, protect-
ing his secrets with his body. "Get out! Go! Leave me
alone! This is more important than you can know!"

"Rhonda Poulan mentioned you'd done a horoscope for
Schulman," I said. "She hinted there were shadowy parts
to it, a darkness that she refused to talk about. And now
she's dead."

"I can't tell you anything. They won't let me."

"The Pentagon?" I asked on a hunch. The file I had
psychometrized before on his desk had hinted at military
matters.

"Not them. They don't know anything about her. It's—"
He bit back the name. I didn't believe much of what Bishop
said, but curiosity can be an addiction.

"Who?" I said softly. "We can find out. You know it.
Do you want us raking you over the coals for the faked
videotape about the Challenger? We can go to the press.
We can get them interested in you just by mentioning
Rhonda Poulan."

"You'll ruin me. They'll never give me another contract."

"The CIA?" asked Barbara. "Some of the professors
have grants from them. This is the way they all talk."

"Andrea Schulman is connected to them. She is! Now
let it be."

I frowned. Bishop worried about two different secrets
leaking out. Something about his own work bothered him,
but he also agonized over revealing Schulman's connection
with the government.

"The Pentagon," I said aloud, as if thinking aloud.
"What do they need with an astrologer?"

"I can't tell you. I can't. They—they'll throw me in jail forever!"

"No," said Barbara, shaking her head. She sat down heavily in a chair. "I can't believe what just crossed my mind. The military pays you to work up horoscopes? They're planning battles based on astrology?"

"I never said that," Bishop cried.

Part of his secret was out. I shared Barbara's disgust with the idea that the government considered astrology as a means of forecasting the future. Considering how pitifully America had done, from Vietnam on, I wondered how much could be attributed to belief in the supernatural and the influence of planets and how much could be laid at the door of inept officers, training and supply.

"It's lucrative, isn't it?" I asked.

"More than you'll ever make, Thorne," he snapped. "Leave me be. Get out of here. My secretary has already called the police. Don't make them throw you into jail."

"Andrea Schulman," I said, keeping him off balance. "Rhonda Poulan mentioned her horoscope. Is she your link with the Pentagon?"

"I don't know about her. I don't. She works for one of the spook groups."

"Her horoscope told you that?" Barbara's contempt dripped from every word.

"It was her multiple birthday," Bishop said, then looked frightened.

"One is the usual number," I said.

"She's forty-three, but her 'scope reads as if she were only fifteen," he said. "I can't say anymore about it. I can't."

"Won't, you mean," Barbara stood and glared at Bishop. Hard. We had him off balance now that his secrets were coming into the light of day.

"How involved were you and Priscilla Santorini in her import-export business?"

"Andrea's?"

"Priscilla Santorini's," I said.

"I don't know what you're talking about. Priscilla was a parasite. I was never sure where she got her money, but I had my suspicions. She was such a typical Leo."

"What do you mean by that?" Barbara knew little about astrology and didn't care to learn. Her question was more reflex than anything else.

Bishop shrugged. He touched a key on the board and the monitor winked and went blank. He was starting to regain his usual poise. Whatever we got from him from now on would be whatever he wanted to reveal, not what we shocked from him.

"Leos demand to be in the spotlight all the time. Vain, fickle, sensation-seekers. Shallow people. They can talk about themselves all day long but know nothing of what's going on around them. Priscilla was certainly all that."

"But her business . . ." I let the question trail off to keep Bishop talking.

"She was terrible at business. Benjamin Larson did it all for her. She was a shrew, a taker, not a giver. Those were her specialties."

"Could she have been a blackmailer?" Barbara asked.

"She might have done something like that. She dealt in power. If it gave her control of someone else, she'd do it."

"Did she use that on you?" I asked. An idea was forming. If Santorini had blackmailed Rhonda Poulan, she might also have been shaking down Bishop. To lose a major government contract for casting the horoscope for World War III would be worth thousands and thousands.

"Hardly. I reveal nothing of myself. My job is to reveal what the stars say about others."

"Such as Rhonda Poulan's lesbian affair with Santorini? Maybe *you* were the blackmailer," Barbara said. She had calmed down and was now taking a spiteful glee in baiting Bishop. I wasn't sure I liked this any better on her part.

"I don't doubt Priscilla was capable of any sexual combination. She was a Leo, after all, and had no concept of morality other than how it applied to her. You might even say she was a sociopath. Right and wrong had no meaning, only winning."

"You *knew* of her affair with Mrs. Poulan?"

"No," Bishop said. The way he said it made me believe him. I was beginning to wonder how their twisted social set had ever come about. No one much liked anyone else.

The ones who weren't openly contemptuous of the others were having sexual affairs based on fear and blackmail.

"But it doesn't surprise you?"

"Only that Rhonda was involved. And even this isn't too startling. She was a weak person, searching for something she wasn't going to find."

"And what did the stars say she was hunting?" Barbara asked.

"Someone to tell her everything was all right. She needed a strong power figure in her life. Rhonda was a follower and gravitated toward strength, as if she could suck up some of it for herself. She couldn't. She only got hurt."

"By Priscilla? Enough to want to kill her?"

"Rhonda couldn't hurt anyone. That was her major failing."

Nietzsche would have loved Damien Bishop. "I'm still interested in Santorini's import-export business."

"There wasn't one. She didn't know the first thing about international trade," said Bishop. He swung around and stared out his large window at the city sprawled below. "She had no taste whatsoever in decorating. Or at least her personality matched her tastes—all chrome and sharp edges."

"She wasn't an expert on Japanese art?"

Bishop laughed. "She couldn't have cared less. I was at a party at her place a few months ago. Andrea tried to give her a jade buddha as a gift. A pretty little thing. It might have been expensive. I can't say. Priscilla threw it through the back window."

"The one facing the ocean?" My mind began working on other facets of this complex diamond problem.

"I doubt she reached the Pacific with it. She didn't have much of a pitching arm."

Barbara started to say more, but I waved my hand. We left Damien Bishop's office. The astrologer never turned in his chair. And that was fine with me. I didn't care if I ever saw him again.

Dottan had recorded the blackmail message. There's a wealth of possibilities to tie her in with the deaths. But it was a man who had started Worthington. He

CHAPTER TWENTY-SIX

CHAPTER TWENTY-SIX

"He's guilty as hell. He did it. I don't know how he made the contact, but men like him can always find a way."

I looked at Barbara and wondered what she was talking about. Her loud words had shaken me free of my own reverie. We stood on the street outside the building where Damien Bishop's office looked out over San Francisco.

"You think Bishop killed Rhonda Poulan? Or had her killed?"

"He could have. All that talk about Priscilla Santorini being a Leo and a sociopath—that's his own personality talking. He did it. I know it!"

"I don't think so," I said slowly, trying to put my thoughts into a coherent order. Everything flowed around me. I felt like Liza crossing the ice floes. A misstep and I'd plunge into a freezing river or be crushed by the very floes I needed for safety.

"He's a crook. You know that. The Challenger tape proves it. And you caught him on the contract from the Pentagon. I can't believe it! He's casting horoscopes for the Army!"

"For someone in the Pentagon," I said. "What branch I couldn't tell. Does it matter?"

"They are fools wasting taxpayers' money on thieves like Bishop," she muttered. I understood some of her anger. She had difficulty getting money for her research project and Damien Bishop was handed who knows how much for dabbling in astrology.

I started walking, Barbara following. My thoughts swirled in a vortex, sucking me toward the center. I wanted to see what was in the middle of this maelstrom—and I feared it. Someone had killed Priscilla Santorini and Rhonda Poulan and had tried to kill Barbara and me because of what I'd discovered. The worst part of it was not having the slightest idea what I had uncovered that meant so much.

Bishop might be a charlatan and illicitly feeding from the public trough, but he still didn't have the *feel* of killer about him, notwithstanding what had happened with my wife five years back.

"She was going to expose him," Barbara said. "That explains everything."

"Who? Mrs. Poulan?" I couldn't keep her from muddying my mental waters. I felt so close and yet she kept poking at me, pushing me just a bit farther from where I wanted to be. For the first time I was sorry I had told Barbara about Damien Bishop and his connection with the psychic healer who had murdered my wife. One day I'd have to find out exactly what had happened to Barbara's parents. But not now. I fought to keep my thoughts in a narrow beam.

"Santorini. Rhonda Poulan doesn't sound like the type of person to blackmail anyone. There wasn't any need for her to, anyway. Priscilla Santorini was going to expose Bishop."

"You've got quite a thing about Bishop," I said. "You ought to keep it under control." I wasn't fond of the astrologer but had come to grips with my own emotions over the years. I just hoped Barbara knew how serious a murder accusation was. Pointing the finger at the wrong man was only part of the problem. If the police and District Attorney believed the accusation, they'd stop looking for the guilty party. Making the leap of logic that whoever had killed Santorini had also sent the *yakuza* hit men after Rhonda Poulan and me wasn't hard but might be wrong.

The next time I might not be so lucky, especially if the wrong man was locked up and I started feeling more secure.

"I want him behind bars."

"Just for being a fake?" I asked.

"Why not?" Barbara's eyebrows shot up in twin arches. "I never thought you'd come out and defend him."

"I'm as interested in justice as I am in nailing Damien Bishop."

"There's proof," she said. "There must be. Who else

could have killed Santorini? You said her murderer was male. Larson is dead. Hackett isn't the one.''

I shrugged this off. The most worrisome element kept coming back to me that Priscilla Santorini's murderer might be a former lover, one jilted long ago and not even appearing on Cunningham's suspect list.

''It's not Royce Poulan, either,'' I said suddenly. ''There seems to be no contact with Santorini other than possible blackmail.''

My sudden turn took Barbara by surprise. She frowned, then said after a moment's reflection, ''He *was* up on charges before that Senate committee.''

''Not exactly. You heard what Worthington said. Poulan's partners were indicted, not him. He answered the questions about racketeering and walked. He didn't have anything to do with the bribes or kickbacks.''

''He was clever.''

''He doesn't strike me as clever as much as he does blunt and very determined. Royce Poulan doesn't look like the kind who gives up on anything easily.''

''He paid blackmail to keep his wife's affair with Santorini a secret. That doesn't sound as if he wanted to fight an injustice or bring a criminal to justice. He could have gone to the police and tried to do it right.''

I had no quick answer for that other than Poulan had loved his wife and wanted to protect her. Would he kill for her? Possibly. And once more, my reading of his character came more into play than strict logic. Royce Poulan might have the explosive temper needed to imprint the murder weapon with the stark hatred I heard every time I touched the crystal blade, but I didn't think so.

The power locked in the crystal structure stemmed from hatred of Priscilla Santorini—and all women. If Royce Poulan had killed for his wife, there would have been an element of the love that I knew was there for her.

''It would have ruined him after the Senate's mob investigation,'' Barbara pressed. ''Maybe Poulan couldn't have taken the public disclosure of his wife's lesbian affair. His customers would have left his cruise ships in droves.''

''We're all veterans of the sexual revolution,'' I said distractedly. ''The first is damaging, the second wouldn't even be noticed by most people. Who knows what goes on among the echelon of high society Rhonda Poulan and Priscilla Santorini belonged to?" At most, the gossip's half-life wouldn't be more than a month. After that no one would remember or care. Any new tidbit would have upstaged such a pedestrian thing as a love affair between relatively minor players on the society circuit.

"You're doing a good job of claiming everyone's exempt from suspicion," said Barbara. "You don't think it was Bishop. It wasn't Royce Poulan. What about Hackett? Could you have misread him? Somebody's got to have hired the *yakuza* to try to kill us."

"The blackness of his AIDS might hide a lot, but not this," I said. "The stark power in the knife is unlike anything I've ever felt. You experienced it, too. The hatred must have festered inside the killer for years. Something Santorini did or said triggered it and brought forth a stream of fury that no one could live with and stay sane."

"We're looking for a crazy man?"

"Yes," I said. "This wasn't any crime of passion, not like a husband killing a wife. It wasn't done on the spur of the moment." Somehow, Benjamin Larson's murderer and Priscilla Santorini's were the same man. The former death had been coldly executed and the latter had been fiery. Why? What made both of them worth killing, and what made the motives—the emotions—so different?

"You're saying the murderer maneuvered Santorini into triggering the hatred?"

I was no psychologist, but this was a possibility slowly forming in my thoughts and taking on a reality of its own. The pressures of hatred, of self and women, inside the killer had to be immense. He might not have realized he was seeking a relief valve through the murder, but he had. Santorini had said or done something to release the pent-up anger, and had died as a result. She would have stood a better chance playing catch with a hand grenade.

For all the woman's failings, she might have been a victim. I couldn't say innocent and I couldn't say she didn't deserve some measure of punishment, but death?

She had been killed by someone seeking a way to maintain a facade of sanity.

CHAPTER TWENTY-SEVEN

The Marin County CHP office looked like a mausoleum today. The fleet of cruisers I'd seen before were gone; only a few cars dotted the large parking area. I heaved a deep sigh. I'd hoped to find Cunningham in his office, but with so few officers present, it was likely he had gone out on business. There wasn't anything for me to do but try to contact him.

At the front desk, the bored dispatch sergeant looked up. "You again? The Lieutenant's not wanting to talk to you."

"Is he in?"

"You ever read that book? The one about the officer who's never in when he's in, and he's only in when he's out?"

"Catch 22," I said.

"Yeah, that's the one. Well, the Lieutenant's in. You can wait over there for him." The officer pointed to a straight-backed, hard wood chair that would destroy anyone's spine within ten minutes. I had no idea what it might do to even softer portions of my anatomy. Nothing good, I was sure.

"So he's out? When do you expect him back?"

"The Lieutenant's got a lot on his mind, Mr. Thorne," the sergeant said. "And not having you on it is a real pleasure, if you catch my drift."

"I wanted to talk to him about—"

"It doesn't matter. Send him a Christmas card. Hell, send him flowers. It'd dress this place up. But don't try getting in to see him. You're on the list."

The way he said it, I heard capital letters. The List.

"Any news about the Santorini case?"

"I doubt it," the officer said, turning back to his tabloid. Reading the headlines upside down, I saw Elvis had been seen working as a counselor at a fat farm in Oklahoma and that promiscuous space aliens had brought AIDS to the Earth.

"You want this?" the sergeant offered, seeing my interest in his reading material. "I never believed Elvis was dead. Couldn't believe he was seen in a Burger King in Kalamazoo, though. The King always ate pizza, not hamburgers. But this might be the real thing . . ."

"Thanks, no," I said. Who would have thought Elvis would have become the Bigfoot of the 1980s? "I'll be going. Tell Lieutenant Cunningham I stopped by."

"Yeah, sure," he said, and I knew he was lying. I'd be a fading memory before I got to the parking lot.

Cunningham might be on the case, investigating for all he was worth. It had been ten days since Priscilla Santorini died and the knife sang its ugly death song. And then again, he might have moved the file to the "open but not currently being investigated" stack. By this time, the California Highway Patrol had a dozen other felony cases to work on. Cunningham's interest in solving the murder might have been dimmed by more pressing matters.

The BMW started and purred quietly as I pulled it out of the lot and onto 101 heading back to San Francisco. As I neared the turnoff that lead toward the Pacific and Priscilla Santorini's hidden house, I started arguing with myself about pushing the matter anymore.

I argued and lost.

I took the turnoff and meandered through the forest before I realized I had firmly committed myself to seeing this through to the bitter end. Curiosity and a sense of the evil locked within the murder weapon had started me on the case. Someone fearing me enough to hire a professional killer to gun me down kept me going.

Curiosity had turned into self-preservation. I had no doubt that Santorini's killer had hired the *yakuza* hit men. Solve one case and the other was taken care of. And the added bonus would be getting Benjamin Larson's killer. The *shuriken* might have been wielded by one of the Japanese hit men.

The yellow plastic police barriers were still in place. I parked my car outside and went to the drive and looked toward the house. There wasn't any indication the police or anyone else had been here for days. A steady drizzle might have wiped out the small signs I sought, but I didn't think so. A quick look around convinced me no one was particularly interested in me. After all, the house was set back off the road and the nearest neighbor was a quarter mile away.

Ducking under the taut tape, I walked cautiously toward the house. I had the feeling of doing something illegal—something more than just crossing a marked police line. I fought down the feeling of intruding on the dead.

The front door was locked. I checked windows around the side and back; they were secured, too. Peering through a bedroom window gave me a ghastly view of the murder scene. The white tape outline where Santorini had been found hadn't been touched. Other items in the room were rearranged from the way I remembered them. My memory for such things is acute through years of practice and performing my mentalist act.

Even as I congratulated myself on having such a fine memory of odd and trivial objects and occurrences, something began niggling at the back of my mind. I knew something and didn't appreciate its significance. I looked into the murdered woman's bedroom but didn't see it. My mind cast out to more distant points.

I took deep, slow breaths and let a gauzy warmth descend around me while putting me in touch with the higher plane where auras could be reached through my psychometric skills.

Nothing distinct came. A jumble of impressions crowded in. Too many police and curious, careless onlookers had been through the room in the past days. Even then, I didn't think my psychometry skill was the one I needed most. I knew something and couldn't fit it into the picture in the proper place.

I shook myself out of the trance and pressed my face against the windowpane again. The room was cold, stark and as angular as Damien Bishop had intimated Santorini's soul was. Whatever I sought wasn't inside.

Walking around to the back porch, I stared down the slope toward the Pacific Ocean. The battleship gray waves crashed into an unseen shore not far away. Mist sprayed up into the air and came down in a constant drizzle. In the summer, it would be invigorating. Now it was depressing. In spite of that, I sat on a deck chair and tried to penetrate the veil of cloud between me and the ocean.

Images formed in the chaotic swirls of fog, faces and animals and unspeakable demons. Through it all ranged a comet, pulling its tail along with it.

I jerked around suddenly, unaware that I had drifted back into my trance. The comet would have originated in the window at the far end of the deck.

"Bishop," I muttered. "He said Santorini threw a jade figurine out the window." I jumped to my feet and examined the window. It was intact. Only in my mind had it been shattered by the flying buddha.

Turning, I estimated where a moderate-sized statue might have landed. I jumped off the deck and slid down the steep hill, getting my clothes filthy with the slick mud and juicy vegetation. I caught at tree limbs as I half-slid, half-walked down the hillside. When I'd gone far enough— and I have no idea how I came to that conclusion—I wrapped my arms around a rough-barked tree and dug in my heels.

I began rooting in the wet, fragrant mulch on the ground like some tenacious, if not too bright, scavenger. Twenty minutes later, and an additional ten feet down the hill, I found it.

The base of the jade buddha poked up through the debris and gleamed dully. I used a fallen redwood branch to push away the humus. Something kept me from touching the figurine until I got a better look at it.

I couldn't tell how long it had been on the hill, but it might have been the several months Damien Bishop had claimed.

Using the toe of my shoe, I rolled the jade statue over and over. When it started tumbling down the slope, I reached out and grabbed it. I didn't want to chase it down the steep incline.

Bitch!

I dropped the buddha as if it had turned white-hot. Using my digging stick, I kept the figurine from getting away from me. Shaken, I sat on the wet ground and stared at it. The number of artifacts that give me such a psycho-metric jolt outside my trance are limited.

This had the same power locked in it that the crystal blade did.

I closed my eyes and began working to settle my mind. The trance came slowly; I had to fight at every turn to keep from losing my concentration. Anticipation of what was about to come distracted me.

Reaching out, I cupped the jade statue as if it might bite. The power blasted into my brain, its intensity stunning.

Slut! You want my cock, don't you? I'll kill you, you fucking bitch!

The images swirling around with the battering ram of emotion confused me. I gave up trying to piece them to-gether. All I wanted to do was find somewhere quiet and recuperate.

That and decide if Damien Bishop had lied to me about this being a gift to the deceased from Andrea Schulman.

CHAPTER TWENTY-EIGHT

"So what?" Willie Worthington lounged back in his battered chair and stared at me. A speck of mustard soiled his green paisley tie. How he could stand a steady diet of hot dogs was beyond me.

"I had meant to ask him a couple questions the other day and forgot about it," I said.

"It's still that Santorini thing, isn't it? I should never have put you onto Cunningham like that. Getting shot at makes people turn real strange."

"You didn't put me onto him," I said. "You told me to see if I could get anything on Steve Hackett. At the time, I didn't."

"And you still don't. *I'm* getting everything sewn up nice and neat," Worthington said. "Hackett's spilled his guts about the Sexton drug murders. We've got the two dudes who pulled the trigger staked out and will bust their asses any time now. It's taking longer than I'd thought, but we're being careful and by-the-book on it."

"I'm happy you're going to get a clean bust," I said, "but I just want to ask him a couple questions about Santorini."

Worthington gnawed at his pencil, then tossed it onto his desk. "I don't owe you, Peter. You're going to owe me for this one. And if you screw it up by prejudicing Hackett's evidence in any way . . ." He let his voice trail off in threat.

"I don't care about your case. Not even the Larson killing, except as it ties into this one."

"And you shouldn't about the Santorini case, either." Worthington dug through a tower of manila folders on his desk and found one near the bottom. He pulled it out and pushed it across to me. "You didn't see any of this." He heaved himself to his feet and left, coffee cup dangling from a thick index finger.

I flipped it open and saw my name prominently displayed on the typewritten top sheet. This was Worthington's report on the near miss in the street outside the university laboratory. Scanning it quickly, I learned nothing new. The police held little hope of finding the *yakuza* killers. Worthington and an INS agent guessed that the men responsible had killed Rhonda Poulan and driven directly to the airport. A JAL flight to Hawaii might have put the pair of assassins out of reach. They'd blend into the underworld in Honolulu and probably be back in Tokyo within a week.

About possible employers for the pair, Worthington had uncovered no leads. A quick glance at the rest of the report showed background checks on both Barbara and me. Barbara had told the truth when she said she had no foreign contacts, other than requests for reprinted papers. I hadn't thought she had lied. It wasn't like her.

"So you didn't want any coffee?" Worthington asked. I closed the report and leaned back. He was indirectly asking me if I needed more time with the maze of reports and evidence in the file. All I had to do was ask for the coffee and he'd get it for me, giving precious extra minutes to look over the report.

"There's nothing I need right now," I said. "Except for a little chat with Hackett."

"He doesn't know anything about this." Worthington put his coffee cup on the report. It left a brown ring on the cream folder.

"I need to ask him other things. Not even about this."

"Hell, come on. I'll roust his ass out of the cell. You've got to make it fast. You're going to owe me for this, Peter."

"I'll solve a murder or two for you. How's that? Maybe I'll give you Larson's killer on a silver platter."

He snorted in contempt at my easy promise. We wended our way through the ward room, past booking and into the holding cells. The stench rose and turned my stomach. I don't know how they can keep men locked up like animals.

The easy answer that Worthington always gave was that the clientele he catered to were animals. That hardly seemed enough for me and I had told him so. This time, I kept my mouth shut and sucked in slow, measured breaths to keep the stench from getting to me.

"I don't want him taken out of the cell," said Worthington. "And I've got to be with you. Fact is, we ought to get his lawyer—and would, if you insist on him being in an interrogation room."

"I'll ask if he wants to tell me what I need to know. If not, well, this is over."

We went to a cell at the far end of the row of cages. Inside, sitting on the bunk with its thin, threadbare mattress, Steve Hackett stared at the bare concrete wall. He didn't even turn when Worthington rattled the bars to get his attention.

"You want a visitor, Hackett?"

"I want to be left alone."

"We talked at the Charade bar," I said. He glanced over his shoulder at me.

"You were here, too," he said. "I remember you. You were the son of a bitch who said I had AIDS. What do you want?"

I was glad society had decided to stop killing the messenger bringing bad news. Hackett had known of his disease; he simply hadn't admitted it. I had made it impossible to deny.

"You and Priscilla Santorini had a business deal," I said. "Did you do anything more than supply coke for her?"

"That was all. She wanted quality shit for her fancy-ass parties. I've already copped to that." He turned away, his eyes unfocused and fixed at the infinity beyond the concrete wall.

"Did you ever have an affair with her?"

"You mean did I ever fuck her? Hell, no. Would have liked to, but I never did."

I tried to decide what Hackett meant by that. From her pictures, Santorini had been stunningly beautiful. Was Hackett saying he had desired her—or was he saying he had hated her enough to give her the same disease that was turning his body's immune system against him even as he sat in the cell?

What he meant no longer mattered. I knew I wouldn't be allowed too much more time with him. I asked the important question.

"What was your connection with Andrea Schulman?"

"Her? The same. She's a user. All those high-powered bitches are."

"I saw you leaving her apartment a few days ago. Were you delivering drugs to her then?"

"She had invited me over for tea." Hackett laughed harshly. "Can you believe that? She invited me over for goddamn tea."

"And?"

"And nothing. She wasn't trying to hustle me. She's a good enough looking broad. If she'd made a play for me, I might have been interested, but I doubt it."

"Because of AIDS?"

He gave me a withering look. "Hell, no. She's not my type. Or should I say, I'm not hers—I'm male."

"Andrea Schulman is lesbian?"

The harsh laugh told me the answer. I looked at Worthington, who was boring holes in me with his eyes. He started to ask what I was digging for, then bit back the question. We left Hackett to his private perdition.

I was never as glad to reach freedom and fresh air as I was on leaving the cell block.

CHAPTER TWENTY-NINE

"Is there any chance I might look at the items in Property?" I asked Willie Worthington.

The detective gave me a look designed to melt steel as he tried to fathom the reason for my asking. Telling him what I wanted would only bring refusal. Worthington liked me; we had worked together enough times to form something of a friendship, but he was still a policeman. He would never let me have what I wanted simply because I asked.

"I've been more than fair with you, Peter. What's going on?"

"You have something in Property from the Rhonda Poulan killing I want to look at again."

"We've got damned little down there, but you can give it a once over." He heaved himself out of the squeaking chair and forced his way through the squad room, forming a wake of disturbance as he went. I followed, settling my nerves. Worthington would have me in the cell next to Steve Hackett if he found out what I was about to do.

"Jake?" Worthington called, when we got to the basement where the steel wire fence separated mere mortals from evidence in criminal cases. "You back there jerking off or you got a woman this time?"

"Detective Worthington, how nice to see you again," came the sarcastic whine from the rear of the large room. A wizened old man limped up and stared at us from the safety of the steel cage. "What can I do for you? Show you a loaded gun?"

"Stick it in—" Worthington cut off his insult. He turned and said, as much to Jake as to me, "This miserable excuse for a human being lost evidence in three capital cases last year. The captain put it on me when we had to let three fucking murderers go scot-free."

"Too bad you didn't give it to me marked right, Detective."

I cleared my throat. Politics and personal animosity aside, I felt time crushing in on me. I had to see what had been put aside in the Poulan killing.

"Willie?" I asked. "Could I see the evidence in the case?"

"The Poulan killing," Worthington barked to Jake. "If you haven't lost it, too."

"Why, no, Detective. Everything here was properly labeled before being shoved under my door."

"I'd love to shove you—" Worthington bit back still another insult. "Let me sign for the envelope, then."

It took the limping property master fifteen minutes to return with a single large brown envelope. He made sure Worthington signed four different pink and yellow and green and white forms before sliding it through the hole in the wire gate. Worthington snatched it away and shoved it into my hand.

"Be quick about it. I don't like the company down here."

Jake said something about finally agreeing with a highfalutin detective, adding an insult of his own that I missed. My attention fixed completely on the envelope. I went to a pair of chairs against the far wall. I sat in one and dumped the contents on the other.

The victim's jewelry was in the envelope, as were plastic bags of shell casings and her key ring. I held up the key ring and dangled it before my eyes. I ran my finger over the notched edges.

"What are you looking for?" asked Worthington. He had let me get the evidence out of the property room to see what interested me most. "Are you going to do your trick on something?"

"I was," I said, dropping the keys back to the chair with a loud clatter. "There's not enough energy coming off any of this to give me a clear picture. I'd thought I might get a better idea about Royce Poulan and how his wife felt about him. I was wrong." I shoveled the jewelry, keys and casings back into the envelope and handed it to Worthington.

I dejectedly thrust my hands into my pockets.

He glanced into the envelope, then snorted in disgust at having wasted his time. He was furious by the time he rechecked the envelope with the uncooperative Jake.

As we went up the stairs, Worthington said, "He really burns me. He was a good cop once. He got shot up, his leg shattered. For some reason he blames me because I was the first one answering the call. There wasn't shit I could do—it was all over but the bleeding."

"If he's intentionally losing evidence, you ought to make some sort of peace with him," I suggested.

"Heaven knows I've tried. I even offered to bring him lunch. What kind of homunculus hates hot dogs?"

"One with good taste," I said, my mind beginning to wander. Hands still thrust into my pockets, fingers wrapped around the key I had filched from Rhonda Poulan's key ring, I bid Worthington goodbye and left. I heard his grumbling all the way across the marble floor of the lobby. Only when I got out the front door did his voice fade enough to be lost in the low hum of traffic.

CHAPTER THIRTY

"Peter, wait!" The voice stopped me in my tracks, even though I was lost in deep thought about what I had to do. I turned and saw Barbara running toward me. "I'm so glad I caught you." She came up, breathless. She threw her arms around my neck and gave me a kiss that left me almost as breathless.

"I'm glad to see you, too," I said, pushing her away with some reluctance. "I've got to—"

"Can't it wait? This is important. Dr. Michaelson has to talk to you."

"I'm not wearing that monitoring getup again, no matter what you found," I flared. "The damned electrodes itched."

"Please, I think I've convinced him to give it one more try."

"I've got more important things to do. Sorry, Doc." I blinked. I had started calling Barbara "Doc" just as Worthington did. Being around a cop did things to the way I looked at the world.

My hesitation caused Barbara to worry. She put her hand on my cheek. "What's wrong, Peter? You're not telling me something."

I didn't make any cracks about her being a psychic. "I'm on my way to an important meeting." I glanced at my watch. It was a little past five. I wanted to beat rush hour traffic if I could. My quarry wasn't going to wait forever for me.

"What is it? I'm going with you."

"No!"

"You've figured out who killed Santorini, haven't you?" Her eyes bored into me.

"Not exactly, but I know how to find out who did. There are still some things that confuse me about this. My abilities aren't usually so wrong. And the answer I've come up with is too outrageous for me to seriously consider.''

"The knife?''

"Something went wrong when I touched it. Maybe the power locked in its crystal structure was too much for me. I've never endured such psychic strength before.''

"I want to come with you. This is *dangerous!*''

"I might be wrong. I might be on the wrong track entirely.''

"But you don't think so. There's a certainty in your voice, Peter. You can't hide it from me.''

"You're right about one thing. This is likely to be dangerous, and I don't want you getting hurt.''

"I'm a big girl.''

"Yeah,'' I said, smiling wolfishly. "I noticed.''

"And you're acting like a spoiled, willful child. Worse! You're being a chauvinist! Have you told your detective friend? What about Lieutenant Cunningham?''

"What I know from psychometrizing isn't evidence. I'm going to get proof now.'' I looked at my watch again.

"I won't let you go alone.''

I took a deep breath. "Barbara, do you remember the fleeting touch you felt when we were on the astral plane? The message you got from the scream?''

"Agony,'' she said, shivering at the memory. "And hate. It was black and boiling and terrified me.''

"You got only a fraction of its full force. The murderer hates women more than you can ever imagine. The sight of you with me will ruin any chance I have of getting concrete evidence. I can psychometrize all I want. That's no good in court.''

"You can't go wherever it is alone! I won't let you!'' She calmed a little. "Tell Worthington.''

"He's mad enough at me right now without being asked to go on what he thinks is a wild goose chase. Worse, this isn't his case. It happened in the California Highway Patrol's jurisdiction, and Cunningham isn't going to come all the way into San Francisco unless I can guarantee him the killer.'' I closed my eyes and touched the key in my pocket.

Nothing. It was a blank because it hadn't been in

Rhonda Poulan's possession very long. But it still unlocked the case. That and what Damien Bishop had told me.

"Won't Detective Worthington want to solve the Larson killing? You said the same man did it."

"More psychometrizing," I said. "And I'm not sure we can prove that murder, even if I'm convinced the same person did it."

"Let me call Dr. Michaelson then. You need someone with you."

I didn't want Michaelson botching up my unannounced meeting, either, but Barbara had a point. I was dealing with someone who had viciously knifed a woman to death, killed two people with throwing stars, then hired killers to machine-gun three others.

"Call Michaelson," I said. "Tell him I know who put the contract out on us. Have him call the police in fifteen minutes. It'll take us about half an hour to get across town. That means Worthington will get there less than fifteen minutes after we do, if he comes with sirens blaring. That should give us enough time."

"Dr. Michaelson will do it, if I ask. But I've got to have a good reason."

"We can supply it. Let's call Michaelson right now and tell him. But we're going to have to hurry."

Time crushed down on me now that I thought I knew the killer's identity.

CHAPTER THIRTY-ONE

"I wish I could afford a place like this," Barbara said, craning her neck and looking up at the apartment building's pale green front. "Do you know what a one bedroom rents for?"

"Ask in a day or two," I said. "There's going to be a sudden vacancy."

I started in. She tugged at my sleeve. "Dr. Michaelson will put in the call, won't he?" Barbara strained as if she was listening for police sirens on the way. I heard nothing more than the clanging of a passing cable car out on Hyde.

"I hope so. He sounded as if he'd be more than happy to call Worthington just to have me tossed into jail."

Barbara gave me a quick kiss that was meant to reassure me. It had more the feeling of a last request. What I intended to do now might nudge drunk driving out as an unfailing way of killing yourself. I wanted to confront a suspect in a murder case and push him into a confession, if possible.

"Even Burnside," I said distantly. "I'll take even Worthington's partner—in a few minutes. Let's go, Barbara. I want this over. The suspense is killing me."

"What put you onto Andrea Schulman?" she asked. "I still think Bishop is guilty."

"It wasn't Bishop." Reaching into my pants pocket, I pulled out the key I had stolen and stared at it, as if I could convince it to give up additional secrets.

It stayed silent.

We went into the building and rode up to the fifth floor in silence. I took a deep, calming breath and thrust the key into the lock on Andrea Schulman's door. It fit perfectly. A quick turn and the lock snicked open.

"Where did you get a key to her apartment?" Barbara asked.

"From Rhonda Poulan's key ring. I'm an escape artist, remember? I have to be able to differentiate between dozens of keys quickly. I've learned to run my finger along the notched side and remember the pattern."

"But how—"

"Schulman dropped her keys when we startled her. I picked them up and returned them. I absentmindedly touched the key and acquired the pattern. When I went through Rhonda Poulan's keys, I noticed the same notches on the new key."

"Why didn't you say something then?"

"I knew but I didn't *know*. It took other parts of the puzzle to convince me what I had learned was right."

"But Schulman . . ."

We entered her apartment. The *ukiyo-e* on the walls captured my attention as they had before. I wandered around, appreciating the fine collection. A Yoshitoshi print in particular caught my eye.

"What difference does it make that Rhonda Poulan had a key to this apartment?" Barbara asked.

"Mrs. Poulan was easily led astray. Everyone, including her husband, agrees to that. Andrea Schulman is a strong personality."

"So?"

"And Rhonda Poulan was having a lesbian affair with Priscilla Santorini."

"Are you saying she and Schulman are, uh, having an affair, too?" The idea shocked Barbara. I saw the measure by which she recoiled and sank into herself.

"If I were a betting man, I'd put my chips on it," I said. I walked up to the dining room and the shin-high table there. The tea set was carefully laid out. Had she finished the elaborate tea ceremony for Steve Hackett? What had she really wanted from him? Was she dealing in drugs as a sideline? Or was she only a user, more interested in having him supply her amounts for personal use as he claimed?

I put my hand on the elaborately decorated tea pot. A sense of tranquility rose.

Ceremony, tradition, serenity, custom . . .

"What the hell are you doing?" Andrea Schulman's

outraged question rang throughout the apartment. "You broke in!"

I kept my hand on the tea pot. More images formed. These weren't tranquil, placid, untroubled.

An uneasy current flowed through my hand and weaseled its way into my brain. I twitched and fought to hold my trance. The uneasiness welling up touched painful memories deep inside my brain.

You can't refuse. I love you, you fucking bitch! Hate! Love to hate you, bitch!

My hand flew from the pot, knocked away by a forceful blow. It took a second for me to focus again. Andrea Schulman's angry face thrust up next to mine.

"You broke into my apartment! You son of a bitch!" she raged.

The impressions I had received spun through my head like a tornado. I caught sight of the images swirling around, but the edges were blurred by the speed, and the overall picture was beyond my reckoning. But the fleeting ambivalent sensations were so much like those I had experienced when holding the crystal knife that no one could mistake them.

"You gave Priscilla a jade buddha," I said.

"What?" Schulman backed off, her face flowing from anger to fear. The alarm vanished and was replaced with a look devoid of expression—or humanity.

"You gave her the figurine, and she threw it out the window. She spurned your advances, didn't she?"

Schulman sputtered and took another step away from me. Behind her, I saw Barbara standing against the far wall, stunned and just staring.

"Or was this the end of your affair with her? She'd had an affair with Rhonda Poulan. And you'd had one with Poulan, too. Were you arguing over a shared lover?"

"She laughed at me. She said I was a freak and wanted nothing to do with me! Her, of all people! She was a whore, a slut who'd sleep with anything, even dogs!"

"Priscilla refused your advances," I repeated, twisting the knife now that I had exposed the wound.

"Yes." The answer sounded like a snake's hiss.

The psychometric impressions fit with everything Damien Bishop and others had said.

"You had the operation fifteen years ago." I didn't phrase it as a question. It was a flat statement.

The woman let out a howl of rage that was more animal than human. She came at me with fists harder than a prizefighter's. I ducked one punch but caught the side of her hand across my windpipe. Choking, I stumbled and fell to my knees.

She rushed me, murder in her eye. I threw myself forward, arms wrapping around her legs. The force of my lunge caught her off balance and we both fell heavily to the living room floor. She was powerful, stronger than I was, but my agility saved me. I twisted free and got to my feet, still trying to suck in air. Rubbing my bruised throat brought some small relief.

"Karate?" I gasped out. "Why didn't you kill Priscilla with your bare hands instead of using the crystal knife?"

"I wanted to see her blood!" Andrea Schulman swung around and caught up the sheathed *katana* displayed on her mantel. The fine steel blade slipped free of its sheath with a sound like silk sliding across silk. She stood, both hands on the hilt, deadly bright blade lifted back over her left shoulder. From the stance, she was as expert with the samurai sword as she was strong.

"I wanted to see her blood. She called me a freak. A damned freak of science!"

"And Larson? What about him?"

"Him! He was fucking her, too! But he knew too much. She told him about me!"

I moved in a circle, eyes on the woman. Her expression changed second to second. Cold calculation faded to bloodthirstiness, and even this ferocious mien changed to total psychosis. She shrieked as she attacked, the impossibly sharp blade cut through the table holding the tea service. It might as well have been a sun-hot laser slicing through lard. There was hardly a whisper as the wood parted under the keen edge.

"You have no reason to kill me," I said, trying to get Schulman back to the coldly calculating mode. Her mood swings worsened. She made a quick, sliding step and brought the long sword around again. Twisting, I barely avoided being gutted. I stared at my chest. A long thin red line had opened magically. A part of my mind wondered why there wasn't any pain. Another part, distant and growing more so by the minute, prepared my body for the death stroke that had to come. But the part remaining inside my body rebelled.

I shrieked, not with pain but outrage. She wasn't going to end my life. There was too much left for me to do, too much to see for everything to end here.

And in this moment came the epiphany. I had always intellectually known what I thought about life and death. Now that I faced death with enough time to think about it, the emotional knowledge hit me full force. The New Age philosophy was wrong. Dead is dead. Die and there's no reincarnation, only eternal nothingness. I wasn't ready for the never-ending dark.

A Viking berserker, I attacked the samurai warrior.

My limbs turned to lead as I forced my way through air suddenly turned to molasses. My vision became acute. I saw every minute detail in the room—and in Andrea Schulman. The sword cocked back. The glint of light off its cutting edge. The sweat forming on her upper lip. The wildness in her eyes.

I pushed forward as time continued to slow and the world solidified. Her mouth opened in a *kiai* designed to strike fear in me. I didn't hear it. I was beyond fear. I had entered a strange space and time where death meant nothing.

In slow motion the sword came around. My brain worked faster than my body could move. I calculated where the blade would enter my head, how it would halve my skull and send brains in a bloody arc across the lovely art prints on the wall.

The death-blow never came. My body shifted back from overdrive and I stumbled into Schulman. We went down in a heap. I fought to get my knees under me, to get to my feet, to counter her swordsmanship.

The blade was embedded in a cloisonné vase.

I looked up and saw Barbara staring in horror at us. She had thrown the vase. Whether she had been inordinately lucky or Schulman's reflexes were so quick that she hit the vase instead of me, I'll never know. It didn't matter. I was still alive.

Then I was flying through the air. I landed hard and skidded. Andrea Schulman had recovered, too. She rose above me like my nemesis. Without thinking, I kicked out, caught her behind the knee and sent her tumbling. I followed her, knowing this fight could never be over until one of us was unable to carry on.

She rose just as I swung a haymaker with all my might. My fist connected solidly with her chin. I heard the dull snap as her head jerked back. She sank to the floor, not moving.

Then I screamed. My hand throbbed with pain from the blow. I might have broken every bone in my right hand.

Clutching my injured hand, I looked up to see Barbara standing over the fallen woman.

"You hit her," she said dully, in shock.

"Damned right I did," I said.

It's amazing how quickly our needs change. A few seconds earlier I had wanted nothing more than to live. I sank to the floor and wished for the pain in my hand to go away.

CHAPTER THIRTY-TWO

"Peter, you're on shaky ground. And if you thought the 'quake of 1906 was big, you haven't seen anything until she gets her lawyers on you. You're going to end up . . ." Willie Worthington snapped his yellow pencil and tossed the pieces aside.

"That's ridiculous," snapped Barbara, coming to my defense before I could speak. "She *confessed*. She said she killed Priscilla Santorini. I heard her!"

"Hearsay, at best," said Worthington. "And at worst, well, I don't want to think about it." The detective looked around the apartment. The brief but fierce fight had devastated its serenity. Several of the woodcut prints had been knocked off the walls and ripped. "You really trashed this place."

"I know what she said can't be used in court," I said, "but she killed Santorini. I know it."

"Psychometry?"

"That and deduction," I said. "She and Santorini either had an affair which ended abruptly and badly or she wanted to have an affair with her. And Priscilla Santorini laughed at her."

"Peter, she's not your run-of-the-mill murder suspect," Worthington said. "Andrea Schulman is chief foreign negotiator for a large U.S. company with dealings all around the Pacific Rim. They can put a hell of a lot of pressure on us to keep from pressing charges. Ruinous to international trade, loss of face with the Japanese, a dozen other pleas the courts might just listen to. You don't have squat in the way of evidence."

"I want them both arrested! They assaulted me! They broke into my apartment! I tried to defend myself when that one attacked me. And the bitch!" Andrea Schulman hissed as she looked at Barbara. If I had needed further proof she had killed Priscilla Santorini, this was it. "I want them both thrown in jail for a million years!"

"Calm down," Worthington said. "We're trying to get to the bottom of this."

"She's not a woman," I said. Deathly silence fell in the room. Then Schulman snorted in derision. "Or rather," I went on, "she was male until fifteen years ago. She started life as a man and had a sex change operation."

"So?" asked Worthington. "It's not being done much now, but there's no law against it. Even if it is true," he added hastily.

"Do your duty, Officer. Arrest them." Schulman returned to icy calm. I saw that she was a dangerous opponent. Memory of her coming after me with the razor-sharp sword hung between us. No matter what, I couldn't let her get away with four murders and the attempted murder of both Barbara and me.

"Benjamin Larson was Santorini's lover," I said. "She couldn't accept that. She tried to make up by giving Priscilla a jade buddha, but that didn't work. Priscilla threw it out the window of her house."

"Yeah, I know. You said you examined it and saw the same resonances that were in the crystal knife."

"And in the tea set, Willie," I said. "She killed Priscilla Santorini. She killed her, then returned and went through the ceremony to calm herself."

"I'd need more," the detective said. "This won't hold up in court."

The officers nearest the door moved back. Leonard Cunningham came in, trailing two other uniformed California Highway Patrolmen. The frown on his face told me he was as unfavorably inclined toward me and my lack of verifiable evidence as Willie Worthington.

"This is bullshit, Thorne," he said without preamble. "If this detective doesn't run you in, I will. You can't break in and—"

Worthington grabbed my arm and swung me around. "There weren't signs of forcible entry. How did you get in?"

I bumped into him. His eyes widened when he felt the key sliding into his pocket. He reached in, then turned livid. But I knew I had him at least half-convinced. He said nothing.

Sotto voce, I said. "Thanks for loaning it to me." Worthington went white.

"Detective Worthington and I worked together on this," I told Cunningham. "He recognized a key from the ring of Rhonda Poulan as being to this apartment's front door."

"What are you saying?" Cunningham demanded.

"There's no way of connecting Andrea Schulman to the death you're investigating, Lieutenant, but that's not true in the Rhonda Poulan killing. The deceased had a key to this apartment."

"That's no evidence," Cunningham said, glaring at Worthington. The corpulent detective's jowls flopped back and forth as if he were a beached flounder struggling to breathe. I knew he didn't like being called on the carpet, especially by a California Highway Patrol officer. "Do you always conduct such sloppy investigations?"

Burnside gobbled. I couldn't tell if he was enjoying seeing his partner put on the griddle or was trying to think of some comeback to give the CHP lieutenant.

"There's evidence, if you care to look for it," I said. "It's not much of a jump to assume Andrea Schulman had connections with Japanese criminals."

"You trying to tie her to the Rhonda Poulan killing?" asked Cunningham. "I'm—"

"The address book," I said. "By the phone. Check the numbers and you'll find one that ties her in the with the *yakuza*."

"I protest this. You don't have a warrant. You can't search these premises." Schulman began to squirm when I mentioned the phone book. What actually was in it I couldn't say, but it must have been enough to start the police digging in the right places.

"We're investigating a disturbance," Worthington said, "and *you* asked us in. Any evidence we find will hold up in court."

"Out!" she shouted.

"Voice analysis might show she was the one who black-mailed Royce Poulan, too," I said, bluffing. I doubted if

Poulan had recorded the blackmail message. "There's a wealth of possibilities to tie her in with the deaths."

"But it was a man who . . ." started Worthington. He stared at Schulman and swallowed.

"The surgery was done, the hormones added, but I suspect she can still lower her voice to sound like a man. When she attacked me with the sword, she gave what could have been a man's shout."

"Get out," Andrea Schulman cried again.

"There's enough to look into," Worthington said. "The numbers in your phone log might be interesting."

"That'll prove nothing. So what if I know *yakuza* chiefs? I know many people in the Japanese community. And you'll never tie me in with Priscilla's death. Never. There's no way you can!"

"She may be right, even if *I* know she did it," I said. "But Rhonda Poulan's death. That's different. She was afraid the woman would tell us about Damien Bishop's horoscope showing the date of the transsexual surgery, her new 'birth' date. She had Bishop too scared of losing his government contract to ever repeat it; he was safe from her. And it wouldn't surprise me if Rhonda Poulan didn't have a hint of information about Santorini's death, too. Pillow talk, Andrea?"

She let out a roar and came at me. I had been goading her and waiting for the moment. Sidestepping, I let her rush past. The woman grabbed up the fallen samurai sword and cocked it back for a killing stroke. Both Cunningham and Worthington had their pistols drawn and aimed.

Andrea Schulman stared at them, then slowly lowered the sword. A sneer crossed her lips. "There's nothing you can do to me. Nothing."

"There's no punishment that will erase the self-hatred you've let build up," I said, "but your mistake was in killing Rhonda Poulan. There were loose ends. After I brushed against you in the elevator before you killed Benjamin Larson and his secretary, you decided you had better stop doing the killing yourself. That's when you went to your *yakuza* friends."

"You didn't recognize me. You didn't get a good

THE SCREAMING KNIFE 211

enough—'' She bit off her angry retort, realizing she had almost given too much away.

"So you were at Larson's. I left him alive. Less than a minute later, he was dead. You killed him, didn't you?"

She started for me again. Worthington is stronger than he looks. He held her long enough for Cunningham to add his considerable muscle to restraining the woman.

"He knew. *She* told him, the bitch! I hated them all! They laughed at me. They *laughed!*''

"Let's discuss this a bit more downtown," said Worthington, his revolver still trained on her. "First, put down the sword.''

"You've got nothing," she said, sneering. She tossed the priceless sword on the floor.

Worthington and Schulman left. Cunningham shot me a cold look, then hurried after them. If Worthington could tie the woman into Rhonda Poulan's murder, he might pick up a few pieces and pin the Santorini and Larson killings on her, too.

For my part, all I wanted to do was sit down.

CHAPTER THIRTY-THREE

"I'm glad they found enough to take her to trial on the murder-for-hire charges," Barbara Chan said. "She was . . . creepy."

I nodded. Facing a woman wielding a samurai sword wasn't high on my list of ways to spend a vacation. That Andrea Schulman had killed with the crystal knife and imprinted her own confusion, self-hatred and outrage at being spurned by Priscilla Santorini only added to my feeling of being well done with her.

"They traced her *yakuza* connections and found the two hit men. They refused to implicate their real boss but saw nothing wrong with making depositions that Schulman was the one they had killed for. Worthington counts this as a major break. *Yakuza* rarely squeal on their clients."

I took a deep breath. "There's not much to tie her with Benjamin Larson's death, though. I'm sure she did it. She almost confessed in front of the police. She thought Larson knew her secret, would figure out she had killed Santorini and want to avenge his lover's death. And Larson would be losing control of one hell of a lot of money with Priscilla Santorini dead."

"Too bad she had to kill him and his secretary. There isn't much evidence Larson knew she was a transsexual, is there?"

"Not much," I said.

"What about Santorini?" Barbara asked. "Can Cunningham pin that death on her?"

"That's doubtful. We'll have to be content with one count of hiring a murder and two attempted murder charges."

David Michaelson came into the lab, looking angry. "The university is up in arms about a graduate student being sued like this. Andrea Schulman's lawyer is still going after you two on civil charges of breaking and entering her apartment. She claims you were responsible for destruction of valuable artwork.''

This struck me as ludicrous. The woman, who had been Andrew Schultz until the operation at Johns Hopkins fifteen years ago, was undeniably guilty of four counts of murder. Worthington was digging through the records and was unearthing other questionable events including smuggling and possibly white-slavery. Worthington thought he had also had a line on dope dealing from Laos through her Tokyo connections; she might have been sounding out Steve Hackett to be her local distributor, though he denied she had ever asked.

Hackett might have told her he dealt only in cocaine and she had dropped the issue. That was another line for the narcotics squad to dig into. The more they looked, the more the police were likely to find to keep her behind bars for a long time.

Capping the mountain of accumulating evidence was Andrea Schulman's self-hatred and her stark contempt of all women.

I wasn't sure if a good attorney couldn't make a case for insanity. That still didn't lessen the impact of having to defend myself against the civil charges she had filed. I had to shrug those off. If she was convicted, and Worthington said the DA was fairly confident, the lawsuit might evaporate.

Until then, Barbara and I could only keep on with our daily work and be glad Andrea Schulman was securely behind bars pending the posting of a million dollars bail. The judge had ruled that the likelihood of her fleeing the country was great, owing to her international connections. With bond that high, she was going to stay put until her trial.

''I just finished talking with Worthington,'' said Michaelson. ''They recovered the jade buddha, and Damien Bishop has identified it as the one thrown out the window. Knowing that story, they might be able to find clues pinning Priscilla Santorini's murder where it belongs.''

''I don't know,'' I said. ''There weren't any witnesses, and Schulman was lucky. The only real clue is the knife.''

A shiver went up and down my spine as I thought of the hideous scream locked within the quartz blade. If Priscilla Santorini hadn't dabbled in New Age mysticism, no one would have thought to call me in, and I wouldn't have personally experienced the mixture of death and anger.

"You really worked this through on the basis of the psychically imprinted knife?" Michaelson shook his head. I knew he still didn't believe in psychometry, but Barbara had convinced him to give me one more try.

"Ready to finish the experiment?" asked Barbara. "I've got everything set up. New instrumentation, new parts of the EM spectrum to monitor."

"What do we do now?" I asked tiredly. If it hadn't been for Barbara's insistence, I would never have returned for this final session.

"Barbara will show you three shovels. Pick the one you picked before," Michaelson said. "We'll be monitoring what's going on inside your head."

This time they hadn't bothered with the pulse, heart rate and other bodily indications. When I'm in my trance, those all level out and remain constant. The only responses they were likely to get were the ones after I came out of the trance. They had set up lasers to monitor the dilation of my pupils, an EEG and some gizmo that I couldn't identify.

"We're ready," called Barbara.

"So am I." I closed my eyes and drifted, forgetting the disturbances in my life the past two weeks and concentrating on the good. Forgotten was Andrea Schulman's warped, killing ways. Remembered and cherished were the moments with Barbara. I let out a little sigh and found the relaxation of the trance I needed.

My eyes opened, but I saw with more than my optic nerves. I placed my hands on the first shovel. Nothing. The second and the third gave similar results.

"None is the shovel you gave me the first time," I said.

"Try these," urged Barbara. Three more shovels were placed on the table.

"Nothing. There's a small disturbance connected with this one," I said, pointing to the middle shovel, "but it's not the same as before. Not as intense a feeling."

This went on with four more sets of shovels.

The first shovel in the next group caused me to shriek.

Darkness descending. Crushing weight. No breath. I love you, Mara. Weight. Heavy, dark, dirt in my nose and mouth, no!

I dropped the shovel and recoiled. Inside my trance, fear gripped my heart. I knew my physical heart beat remained constant, steady, slow. I stared at the shovel. It looked no different from the others I'd examined. But its aura was one of darkness and death. Crushing, horrible death.

"This is the same one," I said, swallowing and fighting to regain my emotional equilibrium. "I'm being crushed to death. God, it's terrible! And Mara. My—his wife's name is Mara."

"He's right, Doctor. You've got to admit it now. There was no way he could have known all that."

"He admits that he's got fantastic memory for details."

"But he couldn't have even known about the accident," Barbara pressed.

"What accident?" I demanded. I had to know what produced such powerful imprinting on the shovel. Death was part of it. But it wasn't a sudden death. It was lingering, awful.

"A workman was cleaning out debris in the foundation of the new psychology building," Barbara said.

"This was three years ago," Michaelson cut in.

"He was cleaning up when the steam shovel operator dumped a full load of dirt on him by accident."

"Crushed, but not immediately," I said slowly. Shivers returned. "He lingered for almost a minute."

"We don't know that," said Michaelson.

"I do." And I did. The man had survived longer than anyone had thought, chest crushed and drowning in his own blood, dirt filling nose and mouth and suffocating him. He had endured great pain and suffering before dying. And his last thoughts were of death and his wife.

"There is no way Peter could have known about it. *We* didn't before this morning."

"This might not be the same shovel," Michaelson persisted.

"It is," Barbara said. "Give me credit for being thorough in this. I traced it back to the work site—and to the man who died. I've got a full report on the man. Listen to what Peter's saying! He knew the man's wife was named Mara!"

"What did you record with your instruments?" I asked.

Michaelson fell into a morose silence. Barbara took longer to reply, since she worked at the computer for full analysis. She told me what I already knew.

"Nothing unusual, Peter. Nothing at all."

Her thesis project was at an end. Michaelson could never approve a topic with such a lack of physical verification. But I know my talents. I have to live with them—and the echoes of death locked in shovels and crystal knives.